Robot Alert

by
Suzanne Martel

**Translated by
Patricia Sillers**

GINN

INTRODUCTION

"This is for you, Adam," said the astronaut, handing his nephew a shiny back box.

"A present from another planet!" exclaimed Adam, peering near-sightedly through his glasses at his uncle.

"What else would an astronaut bring back from a trip to outer space?" teased Alex Vimont.

"Open it," prompted Millie who was already clutching her own present, an extraordinary musical sphere.

But her brother, with his scientific mind, was studying the mystery of the tightly sealed box with great care.

"Ah! Here it is!" he exclaimed, turning a knob on the side. The box separated, revealing a shiny metallic cylinder topped by a second, smaller canister perched on a swivelling neck.

Adam reached out and touched the silver metal. It felt warm and vibrated softly. From each side hung a narrow arm, ending with a pincer.

Slowly the head turned towards him, and the light from two green orbs brushed over his face. From a perforated grille under the eyes, a hollow voice emerged. Speaking French in a jerky way that accentuated each separate syllable, it said, "Hel-lo, A-dam Col-bert, my mas-ter. I am Cy-ber, at your ser-vice."

"A robot!" gasped Adam. "You brought me a robot."

"Your tin man wants to shake hands!" squealed Millie who had prudently retreated behind her mother.

Only then did Adam notice the proffered pincer. He shook it politely, muttering as to an adult, "How do you do, Cyber?"

"I do my best, Mas-ter. Com-mand and I will o-bey."

"Well, command!" urged the astronaut, leaning forward on his cane. That cane and a stiff leg were less-welcome souvenirs of his stay on Amandara Tetra, after the attack on his spaceship.

"I don't know how to give commands very well," said Adam. Finally, he blurted out, "I'm thirsty."

The robot remained motionless, its lights blinking and its arms hanging by its sides.

"That's not an order," explained Uncle Alex. "A machine needs precise instructions."

"I want some water," pronounced Adam, unconsciously imitating Cyber's jerky tones.

Immediately the robot turned and glided towards the kitchen, humming busily.

Suddenly incensed by this intruding pile of metal, Zabulon, the family's golden retriever, began barking furiously. The robot hummed louder and the dog, responding to the robot's secret language, calmed down instantly. His blond tail beat the air and his mouth stretched into his special dog smile usually reserved for favorite friends.

The robot disappeared behind the swinging kitchen door, Zabulon at his heels. Alex relaxed in his chair with a satisfied smile. How good it was to be back with his family after three years. His sister Mireille turned to him, "How is it that the robot speaks French?" she inquired.

"I programmed him myself, especially for the children."

Just then, the kitchen door burst open and Cyber rolled in, carefully holding a yellow plastic bowl filled to the brim with water. Without spilling a drop, he placed it at Adam's feet.

Millie burst out laughing, "It's the dog's dish! Your robot brought you Zabulon's bowl."

"That's probably because it was already filled with water," reasoned Adam sensibly.

"It's amazing enough that the robot even understood your command," marvelled Mireille.

"Next time," advised Alex, "be more specific, or Cyber will lug in the bathtub—or the aquarium."

Zabulon drank thirstily, as if he had just discovered this dish, which was always available in the kitchen.

"Give your robot another order," insisted Millie.

"Shake hands with my sister," ordered Adam.

Before their mother could intervene, Millie put her little hand in the pincer, which shook it gently.

Mireille had paled. She turned to her brother and said in a shaky voice, "I was afraid it would crush her hand. The robot seems to take orders literally."

While the children looked for new experiments to try with the robot, Mireille confided to her brother, "This toy worries me. You saw how Zabulon responded to its signal. It's powerful."

Her brother laid a reassuring hand on her arm. "Mireille, I'd never do anything that could harm you or the children. You're all I have in the world. I assure you, this robot is absolutely harmless."

Just as his niece and nephew were encouraging the robot to clap noisily, the back door

4

opened and in walked Adam's friend Marc, drawn by the sight of the futuristic silver car in the driveway.

"Come here, Marc," shouted Millie. "Meet our new friend, Cyber."

"Cyber," ordered Adam, his face shining with pleasure, "let me introduce you to my best friend, Marc Harel."

With an amicable buzz, the robot glided towards the amazed neighbor and once again politely offered his pincer.

"Hel-lo, Marc Aur-èle. I am at the ser-vice of my mas-ter, A-dam Col-bert."

"Unreal!" cried Marc. "It's a robot. A real live robot."

Meanwhile, in a Vancouver apartment on the other side of the continent, a similar scene was taking place. A redheaded little girl was jumping excitedly around a robot exactly like Cyber.

"Oh, Daddy! It's beautiful! And so polite. Aunt Corinne, did you see how it shook hands with me?"

"A real gentleman," approved her aunt.

"But it's not a boy robot," proclaimed Eve. "It's a girl robot and she says her name is Nootka."

"She can do a lot more than shake hands," said David Kevin. "During the long trip back to

Earth, I taught her our favorite song."

"Nootka, sing for me," requested Eve softly. For three years, ever since the disappearance of the space ship Terra-Luna V, when she had believed her father dead, she had carefully avoided that particular song. Now that the pilot was safely back it would be wonderful to hear that music again.

The robot, in her staccato tones, sang:

Too ra loo ra loo ral
Too ra loo ra la
Too ra loo ra loo ral
That's an Irish lullaby.

It had been the favorite song of the mother Eve had never known. The little girl joined in the chorus, accompanied by her father's bass voice. Even Aunt Corinne, who couldn't carry a tune, sang along in the joyous concert.

Perched safely on a hanging plant, the family's black tomcat Sultan was eyeing suspiciously the strange silver creature who had invaded his private domain. Soon, however, the robot emitted a vibration particularly pleasing to the cat's ears. Little by little, Sultan's fur settled down. He jumped to the ground and sidled over to Nootka. Purring loudly, he rubbed up against the shiny round body.

Nootka, like Cyber in Montreal, had the power to tame animals and make friends with humans.

Both families wanted to hear the details of the returning astronauts' adventures. Everyone deplored the death of Captain Colbert, the father of Adam and Millie, in the destruction of Terra-Luna V. The astonauts told of a daring rescue by a spaceship from Amandara Tetra and of being treated and cured on the friendly Green Planet. And lastly, they told of their return to earth and to their families after a three year absence.

CHAPTER ONE

Late into the night, while all of Canada was fast asleep, the two robots remained wide awake. As the children who owned them slept deeply, Nootka and Cyber silently approached their beds. At this hour no one could observe them, or be surprised that they floated through the air without using the three little wheels that humans thought were essential for them to move across the floor.

They made a muffled humming, and light glowed from their metallic bodies. Each robot stretched its pincers gently towards the children—Nootka towards Eve Kevin's red curls and Cyber towards Adam Colbert's straight dark hair. The children slept on, tossing and mumbling in their dreams. Beside them, watchful, if a bit sinister, the robots kept on vibrating. Their humming increased, lulling the young sleepers.

David Kevin, the astronaut from Vancouver, was delighted to be back home in his extra-long bed. For the first time in months, he could stretch out. He was happy to be with his family again. His daughter was as sweet as he had remembered her; his sister Corinne who was a physicist, as eccentric; and Earth as solid and familiar. Tonight would have been everything David Kevin could have wished for—if he hadn't been aware of the mission he still had to carry out, and that time was running short.

In Montreal, in the Colbert's little guest room, Alexandre Vimont tried in vain to find a comfortable position. He longed for the soothing rays that had lulled him into painless sleep on the Green Planet. From the next room he could hear the stifled sobs of his sister Mireille. Though brave and cheerful in front of others, she couldn't help crying during the night. While Alex Vimont and David Kevin had been rescued by the Amandarians, her astronaut husband had been killed on the same mission. Her brother's return, and his tale of the attack on the Canadian spaceship Terra-Luna V had brought back all her memories.

Sighing, the pilot clutched his pillow and cursed his stubborn bones. Only a few months more, and the Amandarians would have cured him completely. He had returned because he also had an urgent mission. He hoped his sacrifice would be worthwhile.

In a few days the two astronauts, at their own request, would meet with the leaders of the United Governments of Earth. Once again they would plead Amandara Tetra's case and ask Earth to let their benefactors set up receiving stations.

Would they be able to persuade Earth when it was so set on staying clear of its powerful neighbors' interplanetary disputes? With all his heart, Alex hoped so.

Meanwhile, Earth's peaceful citizens were worried about the robot toys the astronauts had brought back from the Green Planet. Had Amandara Tetra rescued the astronauts merely to bring earth under the shadow of its own danger?

Cyber and Nootka, the first ambassadors from that distant world, blindly obeyed the commands of their true masters.

CHAPTER TWO

When she woke up, Eve felt tremendously happy, as if something wonderful might happen. Still drowsy, she wondered, "Why am I so happy? What's happening today?" Then she remembered. "Daddy's home, and I've got a robot!"

She jumped out of bed and ran to the window to open the curtains. It was the same every morning— seeing the huge mountains on Vancouver's horizon gave her a wonderful feeling. As her Aunt Corinne said, some people live their whole lives without seeing a single mountain. Eve, who loved the snow-capped peaks, couldn't imagine that. She'd learned her love of nature from her astronaut father who had travelled all over the world and through the star-filled universe. Because she was an only child,

Eve shared her feelings with her toys and her favorite animals. Bursting with joy, she nudged the big, lazy, black cat with her toe. It was pretending to be asleep.

"Come see my mountain, Sultan! The sun's making it all gold."

This morning Eve was thrilled to have another listener. She added, "Turn around, Nootka! Look how beautiful it is on my planet! You came here in a box and you haven't seen anything of Earth yet."

Obediently, her two slaves did as they were told. Sultan stretched and leaped onto the window sill. He purred and let Eve pet him roughly. Nootka swivelled her head around, the way an owl does. She had slightly stretched the tube that formed her neck, and a little buzzing sound came from her grille while her green eyes scanned the horizon.

Eve carefully explained, "We call those the Little Rockies. The real ones, the big ones, are two hundred kilometres away, on the other side of the Okanagan Valley. But these are high enough for me. That stretch of blue shining in front of us is the Fraser River. The city of Vancouver is surrounded by water."

The instruction manual explained that a robot's brain will record all the information it's given in its electronic memory. Eve had also read that her own little robot could only handle simple functions, but she refused to believe that her toy had limitations. After all, Sultan wasn't supposed to be able to speak English, but she knew very well that he understood perfectly everything she said to him. If he didn't answer, and if he often refused to obey her, it was simply because cats are independent—and Sultan even more so than others—for a good reason.

He was really a prince, imprisoned in a tomcat's body. Eve was sure of this, though no one else even suspected it. Somewhere on Earth, a beautiful princess was waiting too, hidden within the body of a pretty white cat. But they weren't unhappy, because they had kind masters. One day the enchantment would come to an end. Sultan and his princess would return to their castle of a hundred turrets, like the one in the fables of Perrault. Eve had a French edition with beautiful pictures.

Her father or her aunt used to translate these wonderful stories, but now she knew them all by heart. She only had to look at the pictures to recall the tales. And she'd be able to read them in French herself, as soon as she'd learned to untangle the tiresome "le-la-les" of that complicated language.

When Eve had shown Sultan the fairy palace in "La Belle au bois dormant," the cat had placed his velvet paw on the page in a very possessive manner. Eve understood immediately. Her prince with the black fur owned a palace just like that. She showed the picture to him every so often, so he wouldn't mind waiting.

"Come on," Eve ordered and left the room, followed by her servants.

There was a note on the table saying that David Kevin and Aunt Corinne had left very early and wouldn't be back until supper time. Being left alone like this didn't bother Eve at all. Since her mother's death, she'd been used to looking after herself.

Eve went to get washed. As she was about to brush her teeth, she had a sudden inspiration and gave the robot the tube of toothpaste.

"Help me, Nootka. Unscrew the cap and squeeze the tube." She held out her brush confidently. Nootka skilfully removed the cap. The robot's firm, continuous squeezing spurted out an endless white ribbon that drooped over the brush, over Eve's arms, onto the wall, and looped itself in sticky, artistic swirls all over the tiled floor. They must not have used toothpaste on Amandara Tetra!

Eve looked with dismay at the mess. She couldn't bring herself to scold the robot, waiting with the empty tube in its pincer and humming with satisfaction. She explained the mistake and then demonstrated—a bit late—the right way to do it.

She added, "When I do something stupid, I say I'm sorry. Do you know how to say you're sorry, Nootka?"

"I am sor-ry, mis-tress. I am your ser-vant."

Because she was very thrifty, Eve gathered up as much of the toothpaste as she could and put it in one of her doll's dishes. She left a note beside it: PLEASE BRUSH YOUR TEETH WITH THIS TOOTHPASTE. I'LL EXPLAIN LATER. EVE. She and her Aunt Corinne were always writing notes like this to each other. It was fun finding them in unexpected places.

Eve was very late, thanks to the toothpaste disaster. She dressed quickly, gulped down a glass of milk, and filled Sultan's saucer. In a rush, she opened a can of cat food and spooned some into Sultan's dish. Grabbing a banana and her schoolbag, she called to her robot as she left, "Take care of Sultan and don't let anybody touch my things!"

Eve sounded like a general giving orders to the troops. Unfortunately she had forgotten that Monday was the day Mrs. MacIntosh came to clean.

When the key turned in the lock at nine o'clock, the unsuspecting woman was met by a strange little tin creature who waved its pincers and repeated over and over, "Do not touch any-thing that be-longs to my mis-tress, Eve Ke-vin."

At four o'clock when Eve returned, Mrs. MacIntosh was up in arms.

"Eve, I've had to fight the whole day long with this pile of metal. It wouldn't let me tidy your room. We almost came to blows over cleaning the carpet and hanging up your clothes. It hid some of them—and I had to chase it with the broom so I could change the sheets. And come look—just look at what this monster did in the kitchen! Thanks to its crazy ideas, I couldn't even wash the floor."

Eve followed the exasperated housekeeper. On every single black tile of the checkerboard floor, she saw a saucer of milk. On the white squares, plates full of cat food completed the design. Every dish in the kitchen had been used.

The empty milk cartons and tins that covered the countertop showed how generous the robot had been to Sultan. Neatly dodging this abundance, the cat, stuffed and happy, ran to Eve. She was thoroughly puzzled, but then she remembered the instructions she'd given that morning: "Don't let anybody touch my things and . . . take care of Sultan." It's a good thing, she thought, that cats are sensible creatures. Unlike dogs, they never eat more than they need.

Eve helped Mrs. MacIntosh clean up the mess. Together they went to Eve's room where Nootka stood guard over a heap of skirts and sweaters, books and shoes, all piled in a corner. Eve knelt down in front of the robot. "Hi, Nootka. I gave you silly orders and you did your best. Next time I'll explain things better. Now you must give everything to Mrs. MacIntosh so she can finish her work."

Buzzing importantly, the robot immediately gathered everything and dumped it all at the feet of the triumphant housekeeper.

"That's more like it. A pair of tin cans and a couple of tubes will never stop Maggie MacIntosh from doing her work."

An hour later, the housekeeper plunked her tam-o'-shanter on her head—her wonderful beret of MacIntosh plaid with the gigantic pompom—and proudly went on her way, having finished her work with no further interruption.

That evening Aunt Corinne and the colonel roared with laughter as they listened to Eve's story. The physicist had so little interest in household problems that she wouldn't think of making a fuss. As for the astronaut, he carefully explained to his daughter how to treat an overzealous robot.

No one was surprised when Sultan turned up his nose at supper. Later Eve showed Nootka through the house and pointed out particular things in her own room so the robot would understand orders better in the future. Then she sat down at the dining room table to do her homework.

Sitting next to her, Aunt Corinne was totally absorbed in working out physics problems on scraps of paper spread around her. Her team of researchers at the university had come up with a new angle on the major problem of elemental particles. For the next few weeks, the physicist would be more absent-minded than ever, and her understanding niece would have to keep an eye on things for both of them.

The colonel called Nootka and began a very challenging game of chess with the robot. "I taught it to play this game, just to pass the time during the long trip home."

"Who usually won?" asked Eve.

"We took turns winning," said the astronaut. And then he laughed, "I had to teach it to lose—otherwise the games would have been monotonous."

At nine o'clock the trio—Nootka, Sultan, and Eve—went off to bed. While everyone slept, Nootka, gleaming and vibrating, placed an arm over the red hair of the little girl sleeping peacefully under the robot's protection. A quiet humming filled the room. Sultan was purring too, as if in sympathy. Could he have been dreaming of his princess in the tower with the hundred turrets?

At the first light of dawn, Eve's door opened silently. Summoned by an almost soundless whistle, Nootka followed the colonel into his room. At his order she perched, unassisted, on the desk in front of the astronaut.

David Kevin addressed the robot as if it were human. But a witness to this strange scene wouldn't have understood very much, because the colonel was speaking Amandarian. From the robot's grille came a feminine voice — speaking in musical tones — in the same language. The astronaut reverted to English only at the end of the conversation, using the familiar pilot's phrase, "Over and out."

In Montreal, Adam, who was more methodical than Eve, had spent whole days teaching his robot a useful vocabulary. He made it practise all the exercises in the instruction manual — and a lot of others as well. The master had taken Cyber into every corner of his room, teaching it the names of everything he owned. A large basement room had been fixed up for his uncle Alex who always stayed with the Colberts when he wasn't travelling. After the disappearance of Terra-Luna V, Mireille had let her son move into it. Alex now preferred to stay in the little room on the ground floor, so he wouldn't have to hobble up and down the stairs on his stiff legs.

Adam had kept his privacy and his uncle's splendid furniture: an enormous bed which he could use as a trampoline, a desk with dozens of drawers, a bookcase with books on aeronautics side by side with Adam's Tintin and Jules Verne. But best of all was the stereo system that the pilot had generously left for his nephew. There was one other prized possession—a huge white bearskin. The astronaut claimed to have caught this with his bare hands, and told hair-raising stories about it that had frightened Adam as a little child. Though he'd never let on, Adam had been terrified—especially in the night—of this fur. With reflections from the street lamps, it made a white patch on the floor that looked like a monster lying in wait. But now Adam was used to it and the polar bear had become a friendly presence. Nowadays it was Adam's younger sister Millie who dreaded it, because she felt sorry for the poor creature. She pictured the bear, without his winter coat, shivering in his underwear on an ice-floe.

Adam's best friend, Marc Harel, who sometimes liked to make thoughtless, cruel jokes, had suggested stretching out Zabulon's fur in the same way after he died. Millie, who loved her dog, wailed with grief and outrage, and was beside herself for hours, which made Marc feel very guilty.

A stairway led up to the kitchen from Adam's room. It was closed off by a handsome door, padded with black leather and studded with gold nails. For about six months now, a trapeze had been hanging from Adam's ceiling. He envied Marc's athletic body and hoped to strengthen what his friend rudely called his "matchstick-arms". There was also a punching bag, which he often pounded furiously to work off his pent-up anger. This was a trick he'd learned from Uncle Alex who had never been exactly a model of gentleness himself.

There were two windows, high on the wall, that looked out from the side of the house near the entrance to the double garage—the only two-car garage on the street. Ever since Alex had lived with them, the Colberts had needed room for two cars— the family car and one of the famous prototype cars given to astronauts. Lately Mireille's little car had occupied the big garage all by itself. Now it sat next to Alex's futuristic Capra Five.

The Saturday following the astronaut's return, Adam took advantage of his free time to examine, like a good do-it-yourselfer, the inner workings of his new toy. He and Marc were stretched out on the basement floor. They had unscrewed Cyber's top half. Following the instructions in the manual and using the special tools stored in the robot's middle, they had taken apart, one by one, the fifty numbered pieces that made up its brain.

Millie, her dog at her heels, came bouncing down the stairs just as Adam and Marc had every wheel, screw, rod, gear, and circuit belonging to the clever machine spread out on the floor. The boys were studying the clearly marked diagrams. Friendly as ever, the dog went over to lick Marc, but the little girl was furious.

"You ought to be ashamed! Poor Cyber. His head's all emptied out! Adam, how could you do that to your robot? That's the same as if I took Zabulon's head apart. I can't stand to look at it. You two are really mean."

She whirled around and raced up the stairs, slamming the door behind her. Her faithful dog rushed after her, slipping on the shiny floor and scattering the fifty carefully laid out pieces all over the place. The boys looked at each other in dismay. Zabulon was whimpering at the top stair. Marc ran up to open the door for him, calling the dog some very unflattering names. Adam crawled under the bed to look for the precious bits and pieces.

"Girls!" fumed Marc who had no sisters.

"Girls and dogs!" corrected Adam.

After two hours of frantic work, they had to face a terrible fact. One piece was still missing. All the others had been placed on the table, out of Zabulon's reach. Adam's mother had been called to the rescue, and she helped the two boys search every nook and cranny. They found a geometry book and a skate key that had been lost for weeks. Behind the heater Marc discovered Adam's gym shirt and Mireille's sewing scissors, but the fiftieth piece of Cyber was nowhere to be found.

Mrs. Colbert had to give up the search so she could take Millie to the dentist. As she went out, she said, "We'll look again tonight. Maybe your uncle can help you replace the missing piece."

Adam was terribly upset. He'd been hoping to show Cyber to his friends on the baseball team and demonstrate the robot's talents. A shrill whistle at the front of the house signalled the arrival of a troop on wheels. Six boys on bikes swung dangerously into the driveway and almost collided with each other in front of the garage doors.

"Come on," said Marc. "The guys are waiting for us."

"You go. I'm going to keep on looking."

Marc went to the window and shouted, "We'll be right there, champs! Get our bikes out."

Turning to Adam whose worried eyes were blinking behind his glasses, he gave him a push and shoved a glove into his hand.

"You can't do this to the team! You're our best runner and we're playing the Saint-Michel Dragons this afternoon. I'll help you look again tonight." Then he offered what he thought was a sure-fire argument. "I'll ask my mother to speak to Saint Anthony. She always says he helps people find lost stuff. And I've got to admit, she finds everything."

Adam gave in. Throwing a last look at Cyber waiting by the table where the top of his head and the forty-nine fragments of his poor brain were spread out, Adam gave a sigh and followed Marc, shutting the door behind him.

He had a duty to his team, the Charlemagne Champs, and besides, he wouldn't mind showing those smart aleck Dragons that it took more than fancy caps with their club's name on them to make baseball champions.

Two hours later, while Adam was still away, Millie tiptoed down the stairs carrying a tiny gear, no bigger than a ring. She went over to the robot and held out her hand.

Millie had her own nickname for Adam's robot.

"Here, Tin-Head. I found this in Zabulon's

fur when I was brushing him. It's the missing piece."

The sight of the green lights that were no longer lit, the dangling pincers, and the empty head were more than she could bear. Millie was so soft-hearted that other people's suffering always crushed her.

She saw the robot as a new kind of animal, more intelligent than Zabulon, more to be pitied than the polar bear, and capable of feelings. Faced with what she considered a hopeless disaster, she began to sob. She knelt down in front of the silver cylinder, put her arms around it, and drenched it with her tears.

"Poor little robot! You're very sick and it's all my fault, 'cause I let Zabulon come down here. Now you're never going to get better. I love you Tin-Head—you're my friend. Oh, you must have an awful headache!"

The robot slowly raised one pincer and awkwardly tapped the shoulder of the sobbing child. A voice came from its grille, a deep, warm voice, totally unlike its usual jerky one. "Don't cry, Millie. I'm not in pain. You mustn't feel sorry for me."

Stunned, the little girl fell back on her heels. Cyber reached out and very gently touched a big glistening tear that was rolling down her chubby cheek. In its new, almost human voice, Cyber murmured, "A tear! A little girl from Earth is shedding tears for me!"

"You can talk—with nothing inside your head?" gasped Millie, beginning to feel better.

"Yes. But don't let on to the others. It's our secret."

"You looked much better with your top on. I'm going to try to fix you."

Full of good will, she looked at the diagram spread out on the table. "First, rod number 1. That's easy."

By the third piece, things began to get difficult. She hesitated between two circuits that looked exactly the same. Tears again filled her eyes.

"I'll help you," announced the astonishing robot.

Without delay he extended his arms, delicately gathered up the pieces one by one, and plunged his pincer into his head box, placing each of them in proper order with amazing speed. He didn't even use the tools. Millie was delighted and, in her innocence, never thought of wondering about such skill from a machine whose brain lay in pieces all over the table.

At last Cyber took the silver cover and clapped it on his head with a metallic sound. Then, with a flourish, he screwed it down. Instantly the green bulbs lit up. His overjoyed friend kissed him on his silvery cheek. "Are you ever smart, Tin-Head! And you're much prettier now, with your nice green eyes."

"Thank you for re-pair-ing me, Mil-lie Col-bert," replied the robot, separating each syllable, just the way it used to do.

"Me?" Millie couldn't believe her ears. "I did it?"

"You re-paired me," the robot assured her. "With-out you I could have done no-thing."

"Well! Then I'm really glad I made you better."

Zabulon was scratching frantically at the padded door. He'd patiently searched every room of the house and, now that his nose had led him to this room, he was jealous because he heard his mistress talking with someone else.

Millie stood up and asked the robot politely, "Tin-Head, would you like to come up to my room and ask me my arithmetic tables, like Adam showed you? It'll be more fun than saying them to Zabulon. He can't give me the right answers when I get them wrong."

"I am at your ser-vice, Mil-lie Col-bert. Com-mand and I will o-bey . . . if poss-si-ble."

The little girl wondered if she'd imagined the gentle voice Cyber had used to comfort her a little while ago. Buzzing away, the robot followed right behind her, floating over each step until they reached the top. Millie wasn't surprised, even though she'd always seen her brother carrying his robot up the stairs. Zabulon greeted them as if he'd been separated from them for several months. A dog's affection doesn't keep track of time.

Adam and Marc came back at five o'clock, frustrated by their 16 to 6 loss to the famous Dragons with the fancy caps. To make themselves feel better, they raided the kitchen on their way through. Armed with glasses of milk and enough cookies and apples to spoil their appetite for supper, the two pounded down the stairs to Adam's room.

"Where's Cyber?" cried Adam.

"Unreal! Now *all* the pieces have disappeared," groaned Marc. They began to search. From the other side of Millie's door they heard strains of Amandarian music coming from the musical ball that her uncle had brought her from Amandara Tetra. Mingled with the music, they also heard a familiar jerky voice.

"Wrong an-swer. Three times se-ven is not eigh-teen. I re-peat. What is three times se-ven?"

"I don't want you to repeat," grumbled Millie's irritated voice. "I want you to give me the right answer."

"What is three times se-ven?" the stubborn robot persisted.

"I won't tell you!" shouted Millie, furious. "You're nothing but an old tin-head, and you don't even know the answers. That's why you keep asking me."

The little spitfire wasn't making sense. She was startled when her door burst open and her brother stood in the doorway, his friend Marc behind him, almost a head taller. Both their faces showed how flabbergasted they were by what they saw.

Millie was sitting on the floor, leaning against Zabulon, as she usually did. Her blue skirt was spread out around her like a fan and, as she talked, she was admiring her new white sandals. In front of her, holding the arithmetic book open at the page containing the multiplication tables, stood the robot—in perfect condition—repeating in its pig-headed mechanical tone, "What is three times se-ven?"

"Who fixed Cyber?" cried the two intruders with one voice.

"Me . . . of course," came the smug reply.

"You? *You* did it?" asked Adam, gaping at her.

Unable to believe his ears, Adam went over to the robot. He unscrewed its top and looked inside. Everything seemed to be in the right place.

"What about the missing piece?"

"I found it," said Millie proudly.

The two boys looked at her as they never had before—with true respect.

"I found it and put it back where it belonged," she fibbed calmly. After all, hadn't Cyber himself told her that she'd repaired him?

Marc wasn't as tactful as Adam. And he didn't have a sister. He showed his unforgivable chauvinism by saying, "But you're only a girl!"

Horribly insulted, Millie gave him a kick on the shin with her new sandal. "And you . . . you're a big fat creep."

She wasn't afraid to needle him as much as she liked, because it's well known that big boys of twelve don't hit little girls of seven, especially in front of a brother as hot-headed as Adam. Marc jumped aside and kept out of the way.

Adam was shaking his head. He'd seen his little sister do some amazing things—like diving fearlessly from the three-meter diving-board, or finishing a hard puzzle in one afternoon—but this latest trick was not to be believed. To save face, he barked at her, "Keep your hands off my present. You've got your own."

"Take your old robot. He doesn't even know his times tables," she sulked ungraciously. Millie picked up her book. "I like Zabulon a lot better."

As Adam was leaving, he asked, "Did Mama help you carry him up?" He knew from experience that Cyber was heavy, even though the robot always helped him by putting his hands on his hips, to form handles.

"He came up by himself. He knows how."

Surprised, her brother realized that he'd never even thought to ask Cyber this simple thing.

"Boys never think of anything," shot Millie, giving Marc a dirty look.

Cyber floated from one step to the next, ahead of the shamefaced friends. Once they were downstairs, they stretched out on the bed to wolf down their snacks and discuss the disastrous baseball game against the Dragons.

"You know what we need to beat those guys from Saint-Michel?" asked Marc with his mouth full.

"To play better than they do," snapped his friend, gobbling up his sixth chocolate cookie.

"Oh, you're amazingly witty. I'm being serious."

"So am I," said Adam. But then he decided to be more agreeable. After all, he could have hit better himself when it was his turn to bat.

"What do we need to win?"

"Caps," said Marc firmly. "If our team wore caps, we'd play more confidently."

"You think so?" Adam wasn't so sure. But his friend was absolutely convinced.

"Obviously. What you have on your head is very important for morale. Remember how powerful Samson was when he had his hair? When that girl — I forget her name — cut it off, he was done for."

Marc was an expert in faulty logic. It was quite true that the story said that Delilah had weakened Samson by cutting his hair when he was asleep, but how did that prove that the Dragons would be less strong if their heads were bare? Or that the Champs, with their heads covered, would win?

There was only one way to find out: get some caps for the Charlemagne team. Until supper time, when the phone rang and Marc was called home, the two plotters tried to think of some way to achieve their ambitious goal.

Now that this urgent new problem had arisen, Cyber's miraculous recovery was forgotten. Millie, who didn't want her accomplishment questioned, avoided the subject. She wanted everyone to think she was an expert in cyber-thingy, as she called cybernetics, this science of robots that she really knew nothing about.

That night, just like every night since it had arrived at the Colbert's, the robot moved over toward Adam's bed. He came to a halt on the polar bear skin, like a little gleaming ghost. His pincer waved over the head nestled on the pillow, and the servant from Amandara Tetra murmured in the darkness, in a monotonous, even tone.

After lengthy discussions about how to finance the baseball cap project, Marc and Adam reached a decision. They'd put on a show and use the profits to buy nifty caps for the Charlemagne Champs—who without them were champions in name only.

Adam talked it over with his mother and his uncle and Marc asked his dad's advice. The next day, Sunday, the two friends called an urgent meeting of the Champs' regular team members. They were to meet at two o'clock in the "Colbert cave".

There was nothing official about the Champs' baseball league. They had started it just for the fun of getting together with friends from Charlemagne School and other kids in the neighborhood. Their games took place after school or on weekends in a vacant lot. The Champs didn't hold team practice, and the other groups they met from the area weren't much better organized then they were. It was only the Dragons who seemed to have a serious team, and that was because the father of one of their players had a clothing business and was able to have caps made at a discount—blue caps with dragons on them.

When Denis, Big Jules, Richard, and Elisée arrived, the robot was nowhere in sight because Adam wanted Cyber to make a dramatic entrance.

Marc was the last to get there. He had borrowed an old leather briefcase from his dad, and in a mysterious, businesslike manner, pulled out papers and a pencil. Mr. Harel had taught him how to run a meeting, and the boy was well prepared.

"You're not going to give us a test, are you?" asked Richard who was lazy.

"Heck, no! This is the agenda for the meeting," Marc explained.

"The what?"

Marc decided to forget the legal terms. "I made a list of things to discuss."

"Wow! Real serious business."

Adam, who had been won over to the cap project, came to his friend's defence. "It *is* serious, you guys. The club's future depends on it. We've got an idea."

"That's not serious—it's unbelievable," scoffed Denis who was whirling around very skilfully on the trapeze.

Marc tried to get their attention by shouting, "Come and sit down! Jules, put away the Tintin books. Denis, cut out the acrobatics."

It took a few minutes to get Elisée to settle

down. He was battling with the polar bear skin and growling horribly. Elisée came from Jamaica and was the newest member of the group. He owned two first-class bats and an endless supply of used balls— his big brother was a professional ball player. Everybody liked him for his good humor and his ready laugh and he became the mainstay of the Champs.

Denis insisted on remaining up on the trapeze, hanging by his knees. "I think better this way."

"Let him stay there," said Adam. "He's like a salt shaker. Can't work unless he's upside down."

This made everybody laugh. Finally Marc managed to get silence and unveiled the cap project. A lively discussion centered on what color the hats should be, and what should be printed on them. They finally chose green, despite Elisée's protests that he looked much better in red.

Marc, a serious master of ceremonies, declared, "Okay, it's decided. The caps'll be green. Now, what'll we have printed on them?"

Denis, whose face was crimson from hanging upside down, said in a muffled voice, "Charlemagne Champs, obviously."

His suggestion brought a chorus of complaints.

"There's not enough room."

"It's too long."

"Our heads aren't swelled enough for that."

"We'd need foreheads going all the way round our heads."

Marc roared above the racket. "Hey, guys, what we need is a logo."

"A logo? What does it eat in the winter?"

Marc, well coached by his father, explained, "A logo is an abbreviation—initials or a design that stands for our club."

The explanation was greeted with silence. Everyone pondered the problem. Big Jules who was more artistic than any of the others despite his rough-and-ready appearance, suggested, "Two C's, intertwined?"

"This isn't a mushy movie, it's a baseball club."

"Well then, two C's side by side?"

"Marching along together," sang Richard mockingly.

Jules turned his back on them. "Figure it out yourselves then, if my ideas are so funny."

Adam tactfully handed paper and pencil to the insulted artist. "Draw it for us, so we can see what it looks like."

After many silly ideas had been put forward and rejected, and the Champs were no further ahead, Denis—whose cheeks by now were turning purple— decided to come down and examine Jules's sketches.

"Look at this, guys! I think Jules has got our

logo."

He had drawn two C's, side by side, with a star inside one and a crown inside the other. The creator stopped sulking and modestly explained, "The star is to show that the Champs are . . .stars, and the crown . . .because Charlemagne was a king."

"An emperor," corrected Adam. "But it's the same thing."

Elisée approved. "I think your logo's terrific."

"Now," said Marc, keen to get down to business, "we've got to find some money. And we've got another idea."

"Two ideas in one day? Wow! You're overdoing it."

"Even Denis, hanging upside down, doesn't get that many!"

"What kind of an idea?" asked Richard suspiciously.

Because he had thought up the second part of the project, Adam spoke, "We're going to put on a show—an extravaganza."

After a moment of polite silence, everyone seemed to react at once. Elisée flung himself down on the polar bear skin and returned to his epic struggle. Denis clambered back up on the trapeze, and Big Jules, with his hand over his heart, recited in a falsetto voice, " 'The Ant and the Grasshopper', a fable by Fontaine."

Just then, the black leather door opened and a creature appeared at the top of the stairs. Mireille and Millie watched from around the corner.

Cyber glided down the stairs carrying a large tray with pink lemonade, paper cups, and a plateful of caramel doughnuts. His green lights swept over the group and his humming brought instant silence.

Stupefied, Denis let go of the trapeze and landed on his hands. Richard let out an admiring whistle, and Elisée gasped, "Wow, a robot! A real robot!"

Big Jules, however, had been hit in his weak spot, and cheered, "Caramel doughnuts! My favorite!"

"Put it down over here, Cyber," commanded Adam, very pleased with his little success which he'd planned with his mother. He added, "Cyber, pour the lemonade and give some to everybody."

"Yes, A-dam Col-bert, my mas-ter."

"Wow!" breathed Richard, impressed.

The robot placed the tray on the end of the desk. He didn't spill a drop of lemonade. He took one paper cup in his right pincer and offered it to Denis who accepted it rather timidly and mumbled with embarrassment, "Thank you . . . sir."

Adam introduced them politely. "Cyber, this is my friend Denis Lapointe."

The robot congenially offered his pincer to shake hands, but the boy automatically drew back. The metallic arm stretched further and further, as if it would reach for Denis' hand, no matter how far he backed off.

"Don't be scared," Marc reassured him. "He won't bite."

Denis decided to risk two fingers. Cyber squeezed them firmly and shook his hand. "Hel-lo, Den-nis La-pointe. I am pleased to meet you. How are you?"

"F . . .fine," stammered Denis, flustered, "thank you. How are you?" He felt foolish, but couldn't help talking to the little metal man the way he would to a grown-up.

Cyber had been coached by Adam. He answered politely, "I am ve-ry well. All my cir-cuits are func-tion-ing per-fect-ly and it is a nice day."

Big Jules interrupted the conversation. "Does he know how to pass the doughnuts?"

The Champs gathered round the robot, all talking at once, except for Big Jules who was happily stuffing himself.

Elisée had four servings of lemonade, just for the fun of holding out his glass and having Cyber refill it. Then the robot demonstrated his many talents.

He gathered up all the paper cups, added sums, took a few punches at the punching-bag, put a record on the turntable and then put it back in the record-jacket. He went up and down the stairs, clapped, showed them his tools, and unscrewed the light bulb in the ceiling by extending his never-ending arm. He correctly named everyone present, even after Marc had blindfolded him.

Unfortunately the robot had gotten the habit of calling the neighbor "Marc Aurèle" instead of Marc Harel, and nothing could budge him from it. The wisecracking Champs couldn't let this pass. Richard even looked in the dictionary and read out the biography of Marcus Aurelius, "the most virtuous of all the Roman emperors." He held up the picture and showed it all around. "Look at his nice, curly hair. Our own Marc Aurèle has exactly the same kind of hair."

"The only thing he hasn't got is the virtue."

"Never mind, he led us into battle against the barbarians — the Dragons of Saint-Michel."

"He could have done better and led us to victory while he was at it."

Adam wanted to get back to business, so he ordered Cyber to whistle very loudly. Pleased with the effect this had, he self-confidently addressed his now quiet audience. "We have to plan our extravaganza. If we want to make money, we've got to do something that's . . . solid."

"Like a brick wall?"

The speaker ignored the interruption. "Like a play."

"What? You mean we'll have to learn a part?" groaned Richard, alarmed.

"No, we can make up a story and then each of us can pick a character and say whatever we want to," Adam explained. Then he added, as if it were an afterthought, "It's called improvisation."

His mother had taught him the word the night before when they had been discussing the project. The Champs were keen to launch themselves into the theatrical world, and each of them had his own idea about what role he should play.

"It ought to be a science fiction adventure," declared Marc who'd had a whole night to think it over.

"No, a western, with lots of action."

"Yeah! A western," agreed Denis. "I've got a great cowboy hat, a real one, that came from the Calgary Stampede."

Elisée was stretched out on the bedside mat. He announced, "Listen, boys! I'm going to wrestle with this great big furry jungle beast."

"Me Tarzan! You polar bear!" yelped Richard,

doubled up with laughter at his own wit.

Big Jules shouted, "I want to be a bartender—like they have in detective stories. I'll polish the glasses, wipe the counter, and serve the drinks. And I'll pass out peanuts and chips."

"You won't be able to say your lines. You can't talk with your mouth full."

"I'll have a silent part. I'll just listen to the others—and I'll bonk them on the head with a bottle."

"You won't have many customers."

Adam kept his suggestion for last. "We could use Cyber."

"Wow! That's right. Talk about a cowboy!"

"Then it'll have to be science fiction."

"The robot against the polar bear," suggested Elisée who wasn't ready to give up his idea. "That would be a good title."

"Adam, can your robot imitate noises?"

"What kind of noises?"

"Ummm . . .horses' hooves, gunshots."

"Bottles smashing," added Jules, inspired all over again. "We'll do a gun battle in a saloon. . . with a bartender."

"Hey, Big, they didn't have peanuts out west."

Adam looked in Cyber's instruction manual. "He can imitate sounds that you make him listen to—like a cassette recorder can."

"We'll get him to watch a western movie on TV."

"That's dumb," Marc complained. "Here we have a robot and all you can think about is cowboys."

The discussion heated up. Adam again used Cyber to get the Champs' attention. He proposed, "We could combine all our ideas. We'd surprise everybody."

And that's what they decided. There'd be a rehearsal Tuesday afternoon in place of the usual baseball game. Saturday, they'd get the garage ready, and on Sunday . . .the big show.

After shaking Cyber's hand again, the Champs left, bursting with bright ideas for improving their parts.

CHAPTER THREE

The week was given over to frantic prepara-
tions. There was much coming and going
around the double garage whose doors remained
mysteriously shut. By Tuesday everyone's role
had been more-or-less decided.

Only Uncle Alex had been allowed to come to
the rehearsals. His glamorous reputation and
fame made everyone feel shy. To put them at
ease, he piled them all into his Capra Five and
took them out for ice cream. When they came
back, the "ice had been broken," as one wit
remarked, and they got down to serious
business.

The astronaut listened with respectful silence,
his cane at his side and Zabulon at his feet. He
had little to say, and the few suggestions he made
were accepted with good humor.

The astronaut had advised his nephew not to display anything but Cyber's simplest tricks. He warned Adam, "Your robot mustn't attract the attention of curious people or the press. He was allowed to come here only because he was a harmless toy. If anyone were to guess that he's more than that, the army would start snooping around and they'd come and take Cyber away."

Adam, who suddenly had a lump in his throat, asked, "You mean it's more than a harmless toy?"

"It's harmless to us, but you've already guessed that it's much more than a toy. I can't say anymore, but I'm counting on you to keep it secret. Even Marc mustn't know anything more yet. Later on you'll understand."

"You can count on me, Uncle Alex."

Cyber's role would be that of a simple robot and sound-effects man.

The price of the tickets was set at twenty-five cents each, including babies and dogs.

"We'll pass the hat at the end when they're really knocked out by our show," said Marc.

"Wow! Pass the hat to buy caps! Pretty shrewd."

On Sunday, the well-planned performance took place without a hitch. Elisée played guitar and sang calypso music, accompanied by his two young sisters. Big Jules, who had no musical talent at all, gave a very funny imitation of a rock and roll star. Denis executed a virtuoso performance on the trapeze and Marc played the flute.

The improvised western drama displayed the various acting abilities of everyone. Bow-legged cowboys strutted around, their hands near their cap gun six-shooters. Millie, in a long skirt, was a very convincing damsel in distress. Captured by the villain, she was saved by the hero, Denis, almost disappearing under his white ten-gallon hat.

As promised, Elisée crawled in on all fours, hidden under the bear skin. Everybody joined in on the bear hunt, even the audience where little kids pointed their fingers and shouted, "Bang, Bang!"

Big Jules' bar, realistically stocked with rows of plastic bottles, was smashed in the noisy final shoot-out. Millie had stated that she would not kiss her savior, as the girls always do in the movies.

"It doesn't matter," Denis had declared haughtily. "Cowboys prefer their horses anyway. They walk off with them into the sunset."

At the end of the western extravaganza, Adam and Marc appeared dressed as astronauts in silver space helmets. Marc introduced Adam's robot to the audience.

"Cyber, be nice to the Earth people," said Adam with a nod to one side.

On this signal, the robot stretched out his arms and snatched the bowls of peanuts and chips away from the hands of the bartender. Big Jules forgot all about his silent role and began to splutter, "Hey! That's not fair! Come back here! Give me that, you stinker."

He rushed from behind his bar and ran after Cyber who was leaning over the front rows offering the snacks to the little kids in the audience. Jules bopped the robot on the head with a plastic bottle, but it had no effect. He went grumbling back to his bar while Adam and Marc nearly died laughing—as did the grown-ups.

Adam, pulling himself together and regaining his composure, announced, "Ladies and gentlemen, the goal of this evening was to buy caps for the Charlemagne Champs' baseball team. We're going to pass the hat now—if you liked our show, maybe you'll help us."

Adam and Marc held out their round helmets and made their way down the main aisle. The adults and children threw money into the hats and now-empty snack bowls which Cyber held out to them, chanting, "Caps for the Char-le-magne Champs."

Then Cyber whistled for silence, and Adam began to speak again. "Thank you for your generosity, Earth people. Now we have to blast off to outer space."

The robot waved to all the children and beamed a great light over the spectators. Then he left, and from backstage there came a sound of take-off so realistic that the walls shook.

The show had been a triumph, both artistically and financially.

That night the Champs would be able to go to sleep satisfied. If caps were all it would take, they were going to be the superstars of the future.

CHAPTER FOUR

"Nootka, listen carefully. I'm going to practise my scales and exercises. You can record them in your memory and then tomorrow you'll be able to play them along with me. We can practise together—that'll be much more fun."

Every day now when Eve came home from school, she and Nootka made the apartment walls ring with the somewhat discordant sounds of scales played by the pianist and reproduced by her robot. But gradually this teamwork began to take another turn.

"Nootka, please water the plants while I watch my television show."

"Aunt Corinne just washed my hair. Will you brush the tangles out for me, Nootka? You hardly pull my hair at all—you make me feel like purring the way Sultan does."

"Nootka, go peel the potatoes for me. I've got one more chapter to read in my science fiction book. And while you're in the kitchen, would you mind getting me some chocolate milk, dear Nootka?"

"Nootka, be a good robot and tidy up my closet. I have to call my friend Edith about something important."

Humming away, the robot dutifully busied herself, tidying, watering, cooking, while her young owner took it easy. But there came a day when the machine dared to oppose her mistress.

"Nootka, Aunt Corinne's busy. Play the recording of my scales so she'll think it's me at the piano. I don't feel like practising any more . . ."

"No, mis-tress. I can-not."

"What do you mean, you can't? Yesterday you played them along with me perfectly."

"A-long with you mis-tress, not in-stead of you," said the metallic voice.

Without stopping to consider that this logical defiance went against all the laws of cybernetics, the little girl lost her temper.

"It's not up to you to tell me what's right or wrong, you conceited old machine! Go to my room and stand in the corner till bedtime."

Eve expected another refusal, but the robot headed submissively for its place of punishment.

Frustratèd, the little girl sat down at the piano. Scales and exercises streamed furiously from her nimble fingers.

Too proud to call her robot back and caught in her own trap, she knew that she'd been getting away with not watering the dozens of plants that had been left in her care. She had to admit that since Nootka's arrival, the cactus had bloomed, the palm trees had grown taller, the ivy had spread over the walls, and every green leaf flourished, shining with good health.

Aunt Corinne appeared, her glasses shoved on top of her head and her pencil sticking out of her auburn hair. Though she wore a vague expression and was lost in thought, she was making a valiant effort to come down to earth and talk with her niece who spent too much time by herself. But calculations were still spinning around in her head. The problem of abnormality in the neutron's magnetic momentum seemed much more fascinating than household matters.

Aunt Corinne's face lit up with pleasure though, when she noticed Eve clambering up a stepping stool. The little girl was carefully pouring tepid water into the hanging plant baskets.

"You're so kind to my babies, dear. You really know how to look after them."

"My robot's the one with the green thumb. She

hums to them. I'm sure she talks to them in flower language."

"What a lovely expression—talking flower language. All I ever do is tell them equations."

"Coming from you, Aunt Corinne, that's a love song," Eve said teasingly as she jumped down. Then she went to put away the stool and the watering can.

Her aunt was absent-mindedly stroking the fluffy head of a dwarf palm and, totally unaware that she was bringing up a delicate subject, remarked, "I heard you practising your piano lesson, Eve. It might be more fun for you if you asked your robot to practise with you."

"Great idea," agreed the pianist bitterly, with a sullen look.

Then she asked anxiously, "Aunt Corinne, when are we going to make our cake?"

"Cake? What cake, my pet?"

"You know, for the school fair. Edith's bringing one too. We're going to have a banquet. I've been talking about it for a week. Remember?"

"Um . . .yes! I do remember," the poor woman protested, totally at a loss. "I just forgot for a moment. Well, let's hurry and make it now, before supper."

The project, as it turned out, was no "piece of cake." The absent-minded professor forgot to add the baking powder, and Eve got the spatula caught in the beaters of the electric mixer, which bent them out of shape.

"Don't worry, I'll buy some new ones," Aunt Corinne promised offhandedly, trying to make Eve feel better.

The result of their labors was a cake that was heavy, flat, and rubbery. Far too many drops of red food coloring had dribbled into the icing—which was supposed to be pink—before Eve managed to snatch the bottle from her aunt's hand. The dark color was rather disturbing, but only the younger cook seemed bothered by it.

Hit by a sudden inspiration, the physicist pulled a piece of paper from her pocket and groped for the pencil stuck in her hair. With a typical gesture, she peered over her lowered glasses and immersed herself in some new calculations, forgetting all about the dinner, the cake, and her disappointed niece.

"If the neutron has zero momentum," she muttered, "it follows that the particles . . .let's see now . . .."

Resigned, Eve opened a can of spaghetti sauce, threw the pasta into some boiling water, and grated the cheese. Once again physics had gotten the better of domestic chores. But Eve also loved mathematics. She told herself that some day it would surely be her turn to have the thrill of making a great scientific discovery.

That night a touching reconciliation took place between the robot and her mistress. Eve admitted in fairness, "You were right, Nootka. If I want to play Bach toccatas and fugues, I'll have to work on my scales and exercise my fingers. But how did you know that?"

More and more lately, the little machine had been acting on its own initiative. This change had been so gradual that Eve hadn't paid any attention to it—she had merely been delighted by her new friend's reactions. Aunt Corinne, always preoccupied, listened with half an ear to stories about things Nootka had done. The robot had given lessons in French, helped to find mislaid pens, coached the student with her homework, and taken the place of the dictionary by spelling and explaining difficult words.

"Auntie, Nootka put her hand on my dictionary and her eyes suddenly turned deep blue—and ever since then she's known all the words and their meanings by heart!"

"That's just fine! Keep up the good work, my pet," Aunt Corinne answered, not really aware of what she was praising so warmly. As long as the neutron's magnetic momentum hid its secret from her, she'd continue to hunt it down.

As for the colonel, he was tied up all the time

with meetings and scientific tests and never got home before it was time to kiss his sleeping daughter and retire for the night.

Every evening David Kevin placed Nootka on his desk and plotted secretly with the soft, feminine voice that seemed to be the robot's second personality. How would he react had he known that the robot had stood up to its young mistress—and even scolded her?

But the colonel knew nothing about this new development and had no time to hear it from his daughter's own lips. He was totally absorbed with urgent problems.

The two astronauts had appeared together before a United Governments' committee. They had pleaded the Amandarian cause, argued in vain, and set forth the risks that the politics of neutrality involved for Earth.

The heads of state had been firm. The planet Earth, with its scientific knowledge still in the experimental stage and its comparatively primitive technology, couldn'i afford to take sides in the war that was brewing between the planets of the Tetra Group and those of the Worlaks.

Newspapers all over the world reported the discussions.

"Because two of our astronauts were rescued, should we risk our whole planet?" asked the pacifists.

"Better to be friends with the Green Planet than with the Black Planet," replied those who supported Amandara Tetra. There were many of them and they were sincere, but their speeches convinced no one; nor did the arguments made by the astronauts who were accused of favoritism and were suspected of having been brainwashed.

The day after the reconciliation, a very disheartened little girl came storming into the empty apartment. The door slammed, the schoolbag sailed through the air and knocked the head off an innocent little dwarf palm. Terrified, Sultan leaped onto one of the hanging plants and swayed precariously, staring nervously at the young spitfire.

"I hate her! She's horrible! She made fun of me and my cake in front of the whole class," Eve raged at the top of her lungs.

A cat and a robot were Eve's only audience. She banged her fist down on the piano keys, releasing a furious chord.

"Edith isn't my friend anymore! I can't stand her. It's not fair! Her mother helped her. Her cake was beautiful . . .just beautiful. I haven't got any friends. I haven't even got a mother."

All at once the tantrum dissolved into despair. Choking with sobs, Eve threw herself onto the leather sofa, hugged a cushion tightly and cried as if her heart would break. She felt forsaken and imagined herself all alone in the world.

A comforting hand began to smooth her hair. Around her shoulders she felt an affectionate pressure, and a sympathetic female voice whispered in her ear, "Don't cry, sweetheart. We all love you very much—your daddy, your aunt, and I."

Startled, Eve looked up. Nootka was beside her. She was awkwardly stroking the red curls with her pincer, and her arm was extended so she could put it tenderly around Eve's shoulders. There wasn't the least thing mechanical about it.

"Nootka," Eve hiccoughed, snuggling up to the humming warmth of the little robot. "Nootka, nobody understands."

The robot pressed her cheek against Eve's tearstained one. She murmured soothing words and gently rocked the grief-stricken child. Gradually Eve began to calm down. Nootka reached into the pocket of Eve's sweater and pulled out a handkerchief. Then the robot carefully wiped Eve's eyes and nose.

The little girl couldn't help laughing. Nootka's surprising behavior made her forget her misery.

"Dry your tears, my little friend," advised this

increasingly astonishing character. Nootka's voice was soft and musical. "Your friend Edith is already sorry for saying those thoughtless things."

"How . . . how do you know?" Eve asked in disbelief.

"She telephoned to apologize. I recorded the message."

"I was at my piano lesson. What did Edith say?"

Nootka played back the friend's apology, reproducing her voice exactly. Edith had thought she was speaking to Mrs. MacIntosh because the clever robot had imitated that lady's voice to perfection. Eve smiled at the sound of the Scotswoman's accent and tone, and she felt much better after listening to Edith's sincere apology.

Intrigued, she looked at her robot and said, with a little frown, "You've really changed, Nootka! You sound like a pretty lady, a lady with a smile in her voice."

"That's because I'm your friend, and now I can let you know it. This will be our secret."

Impulsively Eve hugged the robot and kissed her hard cheeks. As soon as she did this, Nootka blushed for a second or two, and then her silver color returned.

"Oh!" cried the little girl as she glanced

around the room. "Look at the mess I made. Poor Sultan, sitting up there in the plant! And I broke my aunt's favorite palm!"

"I'm going to bring it back to life," the feminine voice promised, though it sounded just a bit teasing.

The robot gathered up the scattered fronds, put them all together in her pincers, and then attached them to the splintered stem. A white glow beamed from her arms. After a minute, Nootka let her arms drop and stood back.

A miracle! The palm was completely restored. There wasn't even a mark on it to show where it had been injured. Sultan condescended to let himself be petted. The three of them, now consoled, headed for the kitchen.

"Still," Eve recalled as she perched on a stool munching cookies, "Edith and her mother made a much nicer cake than ours. She's so lucky to have a mother . . .and not just for cakes either," she went on sadly, feeling envious.

And then, realizing that she was being disloyal to her aunt who was devoted to Eve despite her lapses of memory, added, "Poor Aunt Corinne— she's no whiz at cooking, but until she figures out her neutron problem she'll never come down to earth. Besides, look at this—she's left her notes and her pencil on the counter again."

Eve pushed the scraps of paper towards the

robot who placed them in a neat pile.

"How would you like it if we learned to make really great cakes together?" suggested the enterprising Nootka.

"I'd love it. I really like cooking, but I broke the beaters yesterday."

"I'll fix them," announced the robot, suiting the action to the word. "There. Now show me the recipe book. I'm going to study it."

Eve put a huge book bound in red leather, on the counter.

"This book has directions, and recipes, and advice. It's too complicated for me."

While Eve put on the oversized lab coat she used as an apron and rolled up her sleeves, the robot placed its arm over the book. The glow from the green eyes turned blue for a second. Then it turned to Eve and said in its former jerky voice, "I am read-y, mis-tress. We can be-gin. Turn on the o-ven to three hun-dred and fif-ty de-grees. Place the rack . . . ."

"Stop it, Nootka! Don't use that cold metallic voice with me. I love it when you talk to me in 'flower language'."

Recovering her feminine voice, the robot declared, "All right, Eve. We'll keep my electronic voice for the others. When we're alone together, we'll be best friends. My real name is Tefla, but you must never use it. Now then, break five eggs into the big bowl."

Eve went to work, guided by the robot's clear and precise directions. While she greased and floured the pans, the robot's green rays beamed over the physicist's forgotten notes. As Eve was carefully measuring the vanilla and her back was turned, Nootka reached for the pencil with her pincer and in one stroke lightly changed a minus to a plus, closed a bracket, and added a zero to an equation.

When the chef turned around, feeling very pleased with herself, everything was back to normal. Nootka was standing perfectly still. The robot suggested making a mocha icing and began to give the instructions.

So, chatting, teasing and joking like old pals, Eve and Nootka managed to create the lightest, most delicious cake that Corinne and David Kevin had ever tasted.

But Eve's aunt wouldn't fully appreciate it until the next day. That evening, as she was about to put some TV dinners into the oven—a last resort on disorganized days—she happened to glance automatically, for the tenth time, at the frustrating equations in the notes she'd left on the counter.

All of a sudden, with a screech of delight, the physicist dropped the frozen aluminum containers on the floor. She adjusted her glasses, snatched up the notes and, with a trembling finger, checked the figures on one of the pages.

"Yes! That's it! That's the key! It's all in the plus. Why didn't I see that before? That's the solution. Professor Tates! I've got to tell him right away. The telephone! Where's the phone? It's unbelievable. I had the answer all the time and didn't know it!"

Forgetting all about the oven and the frozen dinners, Corinne raced for the telephone. No one but another expert would have understood the excited conversation that followed, no one that is, except maybe a very clever little silver robot who was calmly reciting French verbs along with her industrious mistress.

By the dim light of the hall lamp, a ghostly figure in a flowered nightie was wandering from room to room. Eve was looking for Nootka who wasn't in her usual place next to Sultan.

Whenever Eve woke up in the night, she would ask Nootka what time it was, instead of looking at her alarm clock. Nootka's musical voice would soothe her, and she'd go back to sleep contented. But it was midnight, and this time no one had answered her.

She was drawn by the sound of low voices—a man's and a woman's—coming from her father's room. The door was slightly ajar and Eve could see her father seated at his desk, deep in conversation with the robot.

Just as she approached the door, David Kevin spoke the traditional phrase used for signing off a radio message: "Roger. Over and out." Amused, Eve stood in the doorway watching and thought of how she'd be able to tease her dad. This serious astronaut was actually playing with his daughter's robot during the night!

David Kevin shook Nootka's left hand, and twisted it a half-turn to the right. Immediately the green eyes turned blue. The astronaut spoke in a solemn tone, "I wish to communicate with Cyber."

Instantly the metallic voice of Adam Colbert's robot replied in French.

"This is Cy-ber, spea-king from Mon-tre-al."

Eve was so stunned she couldn't move. She felt betrayed by this secrecy between her father and her new friend Nootka.

"Cyber, go get Captain Vimont. I want to talk to him," ordered the pilot in English.

"As you wish, Da-vid Ke-vin," Cyber replied.

During the next few minutes while he was waiting, Eve began to tiptoe away quietly. She suddenly felt like an intruder, very much alone in the world. But her father had been alerted, and turned to catch sight of her sad face. He motioned for her to come to him, then put his arm around her. The colonel put his finger to his lips to ask for silence. Part of the plot now, Eve no longer felt alone.

It was funny to see her robot acting as a transmitter for this French conversation. It was even funnier to hear the gruff voice of Alex Vimont, whom Cyber had just wakened out of a sound sleep. Even though she missed most of the angry young astronaut's French words, Eve was able to get the gist of what he said.

"Do you know what time it is here where civilized people live? Nobody in the world would get a robot to wake up a respectable pilot at three o'clock in the morning."

"It's only midnight here," laughed David.

His hot-tempered colleague's disposition hadn't changed. From the beginning of their friendship, they had acquired the habit of speaking to each other in their own native languages. They both got a kick out of being able to communicate through the robots so that no one on earth could intercept their message. Amandarian techniques were still unknown on the planet Earth.

"I've just received a report from Tefla and Sixe. The situation's getting worse," said Kevin.

He then listed a long series of figures and formulas that Eve couldn't understand. David had lifted her up on his lap. With her head on her father's shoulder, she soon fell asleep. Finally Alex concluded, "Things are starting to happen all at once."

"Yes. We're going to have to get moving on Plan B—and be ready with the third phase, Plan C."

"Right. I'm leaving tomorrow for three weeks at the moon base. You can call my sister Mireille while I'm gone. As soon as I get back, I'll do what's necessary. What about you?"

David Kevin lowered his voice and looked down at his sleeping daughter. "I'm going to arrange everything with my sister Corinne, but I hope we never have to implement Plan C."

"Me too. It's a lot to ask of children. Well, may I go back to bed now?"

"That's a good one, coming from you!" joked David. "Haven't you just kept me up till the wee hours of the morning while you talked your head off? Go to bed then, if that's all you can think about! Over and out."

The colonel grasped the robot's left hand again and twisted it back in place. The blue glow immediately vanished and the eyes returned to their usual green.

The astronaut carefully lifted his daughter and carried her back to bed without waking her.

He stroked the red hair spread out on the pillow, pulled up the covers, and tiptoed out of the room. From the doorway he whispered to Nootka who had resumed her station near the window. "Take good care of her, Tefla. She's more precious to me than anything."

"As you wish, Da-vid Ke-vin. She is al-so my friend," replied the robot gravely.

If Aunt Corinne hadn't had her head in the clouds so much, she'd have been amazed by her niece's sudden new habit of going to bed early. Every night at eight o'clock, Eve went off to her room and Corinne tucked her in. At nine o'clock, Eve obediently turned out her light— something she hadn't done in years. What was going on?

One night Eve had had a daring idea. She wanted to imitate her father's actions. She turned her robot's left hand. Right away the eyes turned blue. Hesitantly she commanded, "I wish to communicate with Cyber."

"This is Cy-ber spea-king from Mon-tre-al," immediately replied the faraway robot.

Caught off guard, Eve said the first thing that came into her head. "I want to talk to your master, Adam."

"As you wish, Eve Ke-vin," Cyber answered.

During the silence that followed, the little girl, appalled at her own brashness, tried to figure out how to reverse the process she'd set in motion.

Then she overheard a strange conversation taking place in Montreal. Cyber was insisting, in his choppy French, "Mas-ter, mas-ter. Wake up. Van-cou-ver is on the line."

"Vancouver?" came the sleepy reply. "What do you mean Vancouver? I don't know anybody in Vancouver. It's . . .midnight, Cyber! Do robots have nightmares? And since when have you had blue eyes?"

Eve was having a ball. Since she could hear the young Quebecker, he'd be able to hear her too. She groped for a few words in her limited French vocabulary and said, "Bonjour Adam Colbert de Montreal. Je suis une amie from Vancouver."

Adam must have jumped out of bed because he sounded wide-awake when he exclaimed, "C'est le robot d'Eve Kevin qui me parle?"

"No. C'est Eve Kevin lui-même."

"Elle-même," Adam automatically corrected.

"Je suis sorry, je t'ai waken you up."

Tu ne m'as pas réveillé, je dormais," answered the boy without thinking.

The two children burst out laughing at this confused remark and then they began to talk, half in French and half in English, making all kinds of mistakes and false starts.

Finally Adam made a suggestion. "Maybe

Cyber and your robot could help us translate the words we don't know."

With the help of these friendly interpreters, the conversation improved tremendously. Curious about each other, they asked questions without beating around the bush. In this way Eve and Adam got to know each other.

The Quebec boy had the advantage of having seen Eve on television. Eve had only seen a picture of Adam Colbert in the newspaper when his family had welcomed Alex on his return.

"You've got straight black hair and glasses?" asked Eve, suddenly remembering. "And you're kind of short?"

"I haven't finished growing yet," protested Adam, very much aware of his handicaps—weak vision and a body that his friend Marc liked to describe rudely as "a physique like a chicken."

"Have you got big feet? Grands pieds?" asked the girl, more curious than kind.

Adam looked at his bare toes and admitted, "Oui. Maman dit que mes souliers sont comme des chaloupes . . . boats, you know?"

No question about it, she must think he was a real goof. He couldn't see how he'd ever been able to make friends with a girl who was as sure of herself as Eve Kevin.

His unflattering description of his feet brought a teasing laugh from Eve. "Well, pas inquiet, Adam. Not to worry. Tu seras very tall, later on, as tall as ton père. Daddy m'a montré son picture. Tes grands pieds are getting a head start. Ils savent . . . they know."

Adam wiggled his toes with satisfaction and felt almost grateful to them for being so smart. He sat up, straightened his glasses, and began to ask his own questions.

"As-tu déjà construit des model airplanes?" This was a subject he knew all about. Little by little he began to feel more confident.

At one o'clock in the morning, Eve was yawning and suddenly realized how late it was. "Oh! Il est tard chez Montreal. Tu dois go to bed. School demain?"

"Oui. Je vais à l'ècole. We'll talk again ce soir?"

"C'est ca. Tonight. A neuve o'clock?"

"A neuf heures pour toi, midnight pour moi. Bonsoir, Eve Kevin de Vancouver."

"Good night, Adam Colbert of Montreal. *Roger. Over and out.*"

Adam who loved this technical jargon, was quick to add a phrase he'd often heard on television, "Message reçu Terminé."

Nootka and Cyber became green-eyed again, and the two new friends went to bed at last, very sleepy but delighted with each other.

Every evening, in great secrecy and with the robots' help, Eve and Adam talked to each other for hours. And gradually, thanks to Nootka and Cyber, they began to master each other's language. Unlike Alex and David who always spoke to each other in their own language, Eve did her best to speak only French, while Adam made rapid progress in English.

After three weeks, they had covered all the general subjects and began to talk about more personal matters.

"What do you want to be when you grow up?" asked Adam, leaning comfortably against his pillows as he faced the blue-eyed Cyber.

After thinking for a minute, Eve answered, full of self-confidence, "Oh! I'm going to be an astronaut and a physicist."

Encouraged by the impressed silence at the other end, she added casually, "I'm going to discover the abnormality in the magnetic momentum of the neutron, if my aunt doesn't beat me to it."

A voice filled with respect replied, "Wow!"

Eve was parroting what she'd heard so many times. Pleased with the effect she'd made, she asked, "And what are you planning to do, Adam?"

Faced with such a display of knowledge and ambition, poor Adam felt at a loss. He'd love to have said that he was going to be an astronaut too, but sad reality stood in the way of his big dream. His thick glasses and his weakness in math were major obstacles to his future as a space pilot. Not wanting to be outdone, he answered confidently, "I'm going to specialize in aeronautics. I'll be working at the headquarters on the moon, like my uncle Alex."

But that night, after they'd signed off, the boy's eyes filled with tears of frustration. He jumped out of bed and started pounding furiously at his punching bag.

Two nights later, as Eve was excitedly planning projects for the two of them so they could be admitted to the space cadet school, Adam cut her off in mid-sentence. "It's no use for me to even think about it. I'm blind as a bat—and clueless at math."

"Oh! That's no joke."

During the long pause that followed, Adam cursed himself for being so frank. It had been more fun when he'd been pretending. Was it because of Cyber who knew him so well, that he'd stupidly blurted out the truth?

But at the other end of the country, Eve Kevin, a very optimistic and down-to-earth girl, took charge of the situation. She wasn't going to give up so easily on her lovely plans for eternal friendship and joint flights like the ones her father and Alex Vimont had enjoyed.

"I can help you with your math. It's my best

subject. And Cyber can give you lessons too. Aunt Corinne always says that with arithmetic, it's just a matter of getting a good start."

"That's not going to fix my eyes," Adam grumbled, even though he was touched by his friend's interest.

"You've got lots of time yet. From now til it's time to get into the cadets, they could make some big medical discovery . . .or invent much better glasses. You could wear contact lenses and not let on to anybody. The inspectors wouldn't even know."

Adam was skeptical, but in spite of himself, he began to be persuaded by his friend's confidence. That night, for the first time, his dreams weren't filled with doubts.

And that same night, before she went to sleep, Eve asked Tefla a great favor—to let Eve see what she really looked like.

A cone of light shone from Nootka's eyes, crossing the darkened room like the beam from a projector. At the center of this beam a figure took shape before the delighted child. A tiny woman, thirty centimetres high, stood smiling, arms outstretched. She was elegant, dressed in a filmy white jumpsuit. Her shoulder-length hair shone like silver and her brilliant green eyes looked at Eve affectionately.

Eve clasped her hands in delight. "Oh, Tefla,

you're so beautiful—as beautiful as a star fairy. I never imagined you'd be like this."

Tefla laughed, the same laugh that Eve had often heard coming from Nootka's grille.

"I'm not really as small as you think, Eve. What you're seeing is a hologram, a miniature three-dimensional representation. In real life I'm as tall as your father."

"Oh, then you're quite tall."

"On my planet all the people are tall. And even the babies have silver hair. Some day I hope you'll have the pleasure of seeing us as we really are. You've become very precious to me, my little earth girl."

"Thank you for coming to visit me, Tefla. Now I'll be able to picture you easily when you talk to me through Nootka. I can tell when you're watching over me. When you're near me, so powerful and so wise, nothing bad can happen to me."

The tiny cosmonaut held out her arms once again and leaned forward to whisper, "Eve, if friendship is all it takes to protect you, you'll be invulnerable."

The cone of light dimmed, then disappeared. Eve found herself looking at the robot whose green rays seemed to caress her face. Smiling, she drifted off to sleep.

CHAPTER FIVE

"Cyber, shoot up to the fourth floor with Mrs. Babin's paper. But don't let her see you or she'll call the police again with her story about a giant monster."

"Ver-y well, mas-ter. But the old la-dy liked chatting with you. She lives by her-self and she's lone-ly."

Adam sighed and undid the shoulder strap of his heavy bag of newspapers. "You're right. Before you came, visiting her was my good deed for the day. But her apartment smells of camphor, and it's so high up."

He took out a copy of *La Presse* and handed the bag to the robot. "Here. Since you insist, I'll go. You can take care of the first two floors."

Ten minutes later Adam rejoined his robot who was waiting patiently by the cart with the rest of the papers he had to deliver on the way home. Adam's eyes were shining and he had a box in his hand.

"Mrs. Babin was waiting at the door with some fudge she'd made for me. She'd have been pretty disappointed if I hadn't gone up there . . . and so would I."

Cyber was very carefully refolding and restacking the papers in perfect rows. Seeing this busy-work, Adam suddenly became suspicious.

"You knew about the fudge, didn't you? How come? Oh, I know—your famous electronic sense of smell, obviously."

"My pow-ers of sen-so-ry de-tec-tion, mas-ter."

"And your powers of deduction, Mr. Sherlock Holmes?"

"El-e-men-ta-ry, my dear Wat-son," replied the robot with mock arrogance. Cyber had been reading the adventures of the great detective aloud when Adam was swinging on his trapeze, building models of space ships, or taking a bath.

More and more Cyber was developing his own personality, which both pleased and sometimes exasperated his owner. For example, he wouldn't make the bed until Adam had tidied his room. He wouldn't ask questions about homework until the lesson had been studied thoroughly, and he refused to spell hard words unless Adam had first made a real effort to write them out.

Saturday mornings, while Mireille Colbert did the shopping, she left the children to do their weekend chores. Millie was supposed to dust and vacuum the living room, and Adam was in charge of washing the kitchen and bathroom floors. But Cyber would only agree to help one of the children at a time, leaving the other to finish the job alone. Millie and Adam had to get used to taking turns with Cyber's help.

On the other hand, Cyber volunteered to fill and empty the dishwasher every time Mireille Colbert asked. This business of showing a preference among chores puzzled Marc Harel who was interested in cybernetics.

"A robot has no will and it can't make distinctions."

"Maybe it can't make dis . . . thingy," grumbled Millie, "but it does what it likes, the old tin-head."

After his newspaper rounds, Adam climbed into the cart and the robot towed him home. Adam, in all his glory, waved politely to each envious child in the neighborhood as they passed.

When they came to the corner of Willow Street, Adam spied the sleek silhouette of the Capra Five. Uncle Alex was back from a three-week training course at the lunar base.

"Hurry up, Cyber! Step on it. I'll hold on."

The robot retracted its useless wheels, hovered above the sidewalk and took off at high speed, trailing behind him the jolting chariot with Adam holding on for dear life.

Uncle Alex told them all about his trip and his stay at lunar headquarters and then he had a suggestion. It included Marc who had appeared, as usual, at the right moment.

"I'm going to take you up to the Laurentians for the long weekend at Thanksgiving. We'll camp out and I'll look at a cottage I'm thinking of buying. It's been years since I've gone to see the fall colors."

"My dad'll lend me his tent," said Marc enthusiastically. "Adam and I can sleep in it together."

"It'll be more exciting than camping out in your back yard," remarked his ungrateful pal.

"Between Zabulon and my white mouse, our night out there was thrilling enough for me," protested Marc.

"I'll do your papers for you," Millie offered.

Adam was just about to thank her when his sister added, "Cyber can pull me around in the cart and you can give me half the money I collect."

"Cyber will be coming with us," announced Alex.

Seeing the downcast looks on the faces of her

two children who thought the paper business was all organized, their mother stepped in.

"I'll go with you, Millie. And we won't charge anything. We'll do it as a favor."

"Okay then," concluded the little girl, "Adam can pay us back when we need a favor."

"Now that's what I call a real family spirit," laughed Uncle Alex. "Millie, if you don't become prime minister, you're certainly going to become a famous businesswoman."

When an astronaut plans to take off at dawn, he means business. The street lamps were still on when the two boys, groggy with sleep, piled into the front seat of the Capra Five. It was Indian summer and a beautiful day had been forecast. When they reached the outskirts of Montreal, Alexandre Vimont pressed a button to put the top down on the convertible.

The fresh air managed to wake up the passengers. Jammed together on the narrow back seat, Cyber and Zabulon admired the countryside. The dog's long ears flapped in the wind. The robot's head kept turning from side to side, and the green ray from its eyes swept the horizon, taking in every detail.

At Saint-Jovite they left the northern auto-route and continued along picturesque side roads. The Quebec countryside was at the height of its glory. From the crimson maples to the golden poplars, the whole forest blazed against the blue sky.

"It's so beautiful," the astronaut murmured with feeling.

"More beautiful than the moon?" asked Marc.

"The moon isn't pretty. It's mysterious, cold, dusty, and silent."

"Is it as beautiful as this on the Green Planet?" Adam asked.

"Amandara's always green. But Canada's forests keep changing. It's as if we have four different forests. Do you realize what a blessing that is?"

"Hey, it's pretty amazing, now that I think about it . . ." mumbled Marc who was slightly taken aback. Who'd have believed an astronaut would have a poetic soul?

Alex wasn't only poetic, he was practical too. Their campsite was briskly set up by the edge of a small deserted lake located at the end of an obscure road. The pilot opened the large trunk of his car and took out a canvas chair which he unfolded and then lowered himself into with difficulty.

He stretched out his numbed legs, laid his cane on the ground, and then declared, "Now then, slaves of Round Lake, get to work. That's what I brought you here for."

The boys wanted nothing better than a chance

to show how resourceful they were and did a fine job of putting up Mr. Harel's tent with its blue sides and its double orange roof.

Uncle Alex had brought the latest in army equipment. After learning how to handle it, you could put up his tent in one step. He also had a very comfortable camp bed.

"I need that for my stiff bones," the pilot explained.

The boys tried to inflate the air mattresses, almost bursting their lungs because they'd forgotten to bring the pump. Sprawled out in his chair with his eyes closed and his pale face turned towards the autumn sun, Alex teased them gently, "Zabulon could do that for you."

The dog was splashing in the water, chasing a frog.

"No, but Cyber could," exclaimed Adam. His face was still red from blowing and he was frustrated because he hadn't thought of this logical solution himself.

The robot not only inflated the mattresses but, with the boy's help, chopped wood, carried it for them, lit the fire, and brought water from the lake. He also skilfully assembled the flat-bottomed boat that was one of the many treasures they found in the trunk of Alex's car.

Then it was time for the picnic that Mrs. Harel had prepared. Marc and Adam had to rinse the cups and plates themselves because the astronaut and Cyber were playing a very mysterious and complicated game. It involved slipping different colored rings over large plastic pegs that were arranged in five rows of five on a square board. Each move required lengthy calculations.

"This is Fala, an Amandarian game," Alex explained. "I got our technicians to copy it. Would you like to learn how to play?"

"No, thanks. It looks too much like math homework," Adam complained.

Marc didn't believe in beating about the bush. "That's exactly what you need. If you were any worse at math, you'd be dead!"

He had hit a sore spot and Adam covered his embarrassment by promising, "We'll learn it tonight. Let's try out the boat now, while it's still sunny."

Alex glanced at them to make sure the boys had put on their life jackets. The pilot was an ideal companion for young campers because he kept an eye on them, but he never gave them advice they didn't need. He remembered his own childhood and knew that experience is the best teacher. He merely gave orders to Cyber: "Go with them."

To the boys he said, "Somewhere in the next bay is the house I want to buy. Look it over and bring me a report."

"Yes, sir," Adam answered, pleased to be entrusted with such an important mission.

The boat set off, zigzagging this way and that until the clumsy rowers managed to coordinate their efforts. Zabulon was swimming behind them in the water, but suddenly decided that he'd rather be one of the navigators. Marc hauled him up over the side, making the boat rock dangerously, though it didn't stop the dog from shaking himself vigorously and spraying his rescuers with icy cold water. After that he curled up at the back with his muzzle resting on the rim of the boat, the better to study the mysteries hiding in the depths of the lake.

In the clear water they could see the slender shapes of trout, gliding slowly by, sluggish from the cold.

"We could do some fishing," Marc suggested. "I brought my telescopic fishing rod. It's in the bottom of my bag."

"The fishing season is over. It's against the law to catch fish now because it's the spawning season," Adam explained. His zoologist mother had wisely taught him a few bits of her scientific knowledge. "If you want to catch trout in the spring, you've got to let them breed in the fall."

Slowly the boys followed the wild banks where the deep green of the cedars contrasted with the burst of colors from the sunlit foliage. In a little bay they discovered the house. It was a log cabin so much in harmony with the landscape that it looked as if it had been there forever. A long veranda overlooked the lake. The shuttered windows seemed like eyes that were closed.

Adam peered at the property, squinting because of his shortsightedness.

"Uncle Alex will be able to land on the beach, and the path isn't too steep for him," concluded the conscientious scout. "Let's go and take a closer look."

They pulled their boat up on the bank and Zabulon rushed for the woods. Cyber waited sensibly in the beached boat.

The two explorers made a tour of the abandoned house. They tried in vain to peek through the worm-eaten boards. Everything looked dreary and rundown. Weeds had grown up through the stairs to the veranda.

"With a good clean-up, this would make a super cottage," said Marc, examining the state of the walls and the roof with an expert eye. Many times Marc had gone with his father who was a real estate agent, on tours of houses in order to evaluate them.

Satisfied with their inspection, the boys headed toward their boat. Adam was whistling for the dog to come when Marc grabbed his arm to stop him.

"Unreal! Adam, do you see what I see?"

Two small brown figures were rolling in the sand and squealing joyfully, under the watchful green glance of the motionless robot.

"Bears," whispered Adam. "Two baby bears. Look how funny they are."

Impulsively he started towards them, but his friend held him back.

"Careful. The mother can't be very far away. Let's get the heck out of here as fast as we can."

Zabulon appeared, bounding along the path to the boat and then stopped abruptly, intrigued by the little strangers in his way. Friendly as always, he went up to them to get better acquainted. Just then the mother bear came out of the woods, growling fiercely and making her way towards her babies with amazing speed.

The dog cowered, his belly on the ground and his hindquarters raised, partly curious, partly afraid, and partly angry. The mother bear stood up on her hind legs. She wasn't sure of herself either, but her fury was rapidly mounting.

"She's going to attack Zabulon," cried Adam, looking around for a rock or a stick he could use to defend his dog. Marc, who was more realistic, whispered, "Let's climb up on the roof. She's between the boat and us."

But his friend, frozen with terror, couldn't move.

Catching sight of them, the mother bear didn't know which enemy to attack first. But there was a fourth enemy she hadn't even suspected, one who was much more dangerous. Cyber extended a threatening arm towards the enraged bear's back. A red beam appeared for a second and the fearsome animal collapsed in a heap and was still.

"Come, mas-ter," called the spasmodic voice. "The beast has been neu-tra-lized for a few min-utes."

Marc poked Adam to bring him back to reality. Adam was still reliving the moments when he'd wanted to rescue his dog but had decided against it. He was ashamed of his cowardice, even though he knew that he'd done the sensible thing. He'd have liked to think that he was brave, and now that the danger was past, he felt disgusted with himself.

Marc had no time for such scruples. The coast was clear and they'd better make the most of it. He headed down the path, keeping as far away as possible from the dark, still shape of the mother bear.

Adam went too, still very pale, and Zabulon, with his tail between his legs, sheepishly followed. Dashing into the water, not caring if their feet got wet, the boys shoved the boat into the water and rowed away as hard as they could.

They had reached the middle of the lake before the mother bear got up, shook her head, and began making her way into the woods. One of the little bears turned around to look at the boat again before he too disappeared into the trees.

It was only then that Adam was able to speak. "Thank you, Cyber. I'm sure you saved our lives."

"I de-tec-ted some threat-en-ing vi-bra-tions. I did not know what this mam-mal was. I did the best I could with-out kill-ing it."

"Incredible!" gasped Marc, throwing a suspicious look at the robot. "Do you know that this toy of yours from another planet is dangerous?"

"It's true," Adam agreed at once.

Though grateful, Adam was also unnerved by Cyber's strange powers.

The two friends looked at each other, not daring to say anything about their fear in front of Cyber. They sped up their rowing. They were spurred to action by the menacing presence of a robot that was capable of paralysing anyone, or anything, with a ray that might be fatal.

Their tiny craft ploughed through the waves, turning now to the left, now to the right, when a clumsy pull on the oar almost tipped them over.

Then they heard the calm voice of Cyber. "You must syn-chro-nize your move-ments. I will give you the rhy-thm. One-two-and-three. One-two-and-three."

With their heads down, the boys obeyed. But the trip across the lake seemed to take forever.

From his chair, Alex Vimont saw the boat approaching flat out.

"What are you trying to do? Win a regatta?" he asked sarcastically.

But the haggard expressions on the children's faces alarmed him. Only the happy-go-lucky Zabulon had forgotten all about the adventure and greeted Alex warmly.

Alex got them to tell him about the drama. As they spoke, he realized that Cyber's intervention had frightened the boys more than the incident with the mother bear. He sat them down, gave them some milk to calm their nerves, and lit the campfire so they could dry out their wet boots.

The shivering adventurers wrapped themselves in blankets and huddled by the fire. Zabulon suddenly settled down and slipped between the two boys. Cyber stood off by himself, as if aware of his new status as a formidable presence.

Alex Vimont brought his chair close to the fire and sat facing the two boys. He looked at them for a long time and then began to speak in a serious tone.

"Boys, the moment of truth has arrived, sooner than I thought it would. You're quite right. Cyber is more than a toy. Your robot is an extraordinary machine, so sophisticated that even I don't understand a quarter of it.

"But the robot is not a threat to you. On the contrary, it's your protector—and much more besides. It comes from a peaceful planet where no one ever thinks of killing or injuring anybody. But these marvellous people are in grave danger; their cities are destined to be destroyed.

"You know the story: Earth refuses to intervene. David Kevin and I understand the danger hovering over Amandara Tetra. And we've risked offering the Green Planet a means of fighting for its survival."

The pilot stopped speaking and put another log on the fire. The boys thought about what he had said. Adam, who knew more about the international situation than Marc because his uncle was so involved in it, was the first to understand.

"Are you saying that Cyber is the receiving station the Green Planet asked for?"

The pilot nodded. "This robot—and the one Eve Kevin has—will enable Amandarian ships to resist attack from the Worlaks."

"Earth is caught between two enemy planets," observed Marc who had heard this many times on television but was now really taking it in for the first time.

"Unfortunately that's how it is," replied the astronaut. "For some years now, the Amandarians have been warned by their spies that the Worlaks plan to destroy their solar system."

"That doesn't sound like an easy thing to do. It would take an awful lot of very powerful missiles," commented Marc.

"In this case, one would be enough. The Worlaks now know how to deflect a tremendously huge star from its course and hurl it at the Amandarian system."

"Move a star? Can they actually do that?" cried Adam totally flabbergasted.

"Their knowledge is vast. Even a small star would destroy anything in its path. Its speed and size would create havoc on every planet it came in contact with."

Alex drew some diagrams on a piece of paper to show the horrified boys how the deadly meteor would pass between the sun and the earth.

"Just as Marc said, Earth is squarely between two enemy planets."

"It doesn't seem possible," Adam objected, concentrating hard on the diagram.

"In any case, this star-missile is already on its way. I learned that from my Amandarian friend Sixe."

"What'll become of us?" asked Marc, suddenly turning pale.

"There's only one hope for Earth, and it comes from the Amandarians. Their knowledge is equal to that of their enemies. They've established bases in various parts of our solar system. Thanks to those, they can estimate the star-missile's path and, by using their entire space fleet, they can head it off."

"The way a racquet returns a ball?"

"It's not a matter of sending it back, but of diverting it into interstellar space. In order to complete their three-way calculations, they needed two receiving stations on Earth. Now they have them."

"And they're our robots."

"That's right. Your robots complete the detection system of Tetra's space fleet. Now she'll be able to defend herself and protect us at the same time."

"It's all very nice to help the Green Planet," objected Adam, looking worried. "But if they lose this war, we're going to have the Worlaks for our enemies."

The boy was repeating the objection made by the United Governments of Earth because he was trying hard to grasp the situation.

His uncle shrugged. "What the Earth people refuse to understand," he explained sadly, "is that the Worlaks don't care about us at all. Whatever side we take, they'll sweep us away like a speck of dust. Their only goal is the extermination of all the planets in the Tetra group."

"And the Amandarians' goal is different?" asked Marc, skeptical.

"The Amandarians are an extremely advanced people who have respect for life and for other people's freedom. We're not only helping them, we're saving Earth."

Marc, only half convinced, insisted in spite of everything, "Then why are the governments still refusing to help Amandara if they're facing so much danger?"

"Quite simply, they don't want to believe that such a danger exists. They don't believe it's possible to play with planets that way. When they finally have the proof, it'll be too late. Kevin and I understand the knowledge these space people have because we've lived on Amandara."

Adam turned to Cyber whose green rays were travelling from one speaker to the other, just like a human listener following a conversation.

"And there are enough instruments inside this little tin man to do everything you describe?"

"Yes, even more than that."

"But," objected Marc who knew a lot about cybernetics, "an electronic brain can't think for itself, and yet Cyber paralysed the bear without receiving a command."

"You've made a very clever deduction, my boy," said Alex.

Adam felt a twinge of jealousy over Marc's quickwittedness, and added, "This wasn't the first time Cyber did something like that. How do you explain it? He doesn't think like a machine."

"That's the heart of the matter," the pilot answered, looking them straight in the eye. "I'm going to tell you something else that must remain a secret just between us. I know from experience that Adam can keep a secret. What about you, Marc?"

Adam was ready to vouch for his friend's loyalty, and answered for him. "Marc will be as silent as a tomb."

Marc was ready to go further than that and said solemnly, "As a thousand tombs."

The two boys turned to the robot, suddenly intimidated by its presence, even though it was so familiar to them.

"Is it an andro . . .an androthingy?" Adam stammered with all the eloquence of his sister Millie.

His uncle couldn't help smiling. "No. Cyber

isn't an android, but his brain is not merely electronic. I'll tell you about him. Somewhere out there," said the pilot, waving towards the heavens, "two small satellites are spinning around the earth, so high that none of our equipment can detect them. Each of those satellites is inhabited by a heroic cosmonaut who, in the utmost solitude, controls the functions of your robots. They come from Amandara."

Adam began to laugh because Cyber had turned red all of a sudden, as if the compliment had made him blush. The astronaut explained with a smile:

"Sixe has a great sense of humor, and now, Adam, you'll be able to appreciate it more. Sixe, I think it's time for an official introduction. Adam and Marc, this is Commander Sixe from Amandara Tetra. Sixe, say hello to your former master and his neighbor."

Cyber gave a very comical military salute and bowed politely. But the most surprising thing was the new voice coming from his grille, a rich, warm voice speaking in flawless French: "It's been a great honor for me to serve you. I hope that in future I'll be your friend too."

"Hello, sir . . . uh, Commander."

The boys were very impressed and didn't quite know how to respond. Adam was horrified to remember all the orders he'd given, all the ridiculous demands he'd made. He'd even made him wash the floor! Feeling very uncomfortable, he muttered, "So Six was playing a role the whole time?"

"A role he was glad to play, I think. By saving you from the bear, he forced us to reveal secrets ahead of time."

The voice of the distant Amandarian confessed, "I was lonely from time to time and that's why I took an interest in your private life, Adam. But I never meant to interfere."

"You sure weren't interfering when you paralysed the bear," replied Adam who was trying to get used to his robot's double personality.

"So," said Marc, suddenly suspicious, "everything Cyber does, and all the decisions he makes, aren't things already programmed inside him?"

A laugh that sounded amazingly young came from the robot's grille. Commander Six explained. "You're right again, Marc Aurèle. Actually, I'm the one who sees through Cyber's eyes. I perceive things through his sensors and make his arms, his hands, and his head move."

"Remote control," whispered Adam. "You must have many dials and levers in front of you."

"I'm surrounded by them. Some day I'll show

them to you."

Young Colbert suddenly had another terrible thought. "I was constantly bothering Cyber. I must have kept you awake an awful lot with all the dumb things I wanted. I'm really sorry about that."

"Don't worry, Adam. We Amandarians need very little sleep. And I always enjoyed the surprises you added to my routine. Thanks to you, and to Cyber's eyes, I was able to learn about your planet and about the way Earth people behave."

Marc couldn't help bursting out with a big guffaw. "Amazing! You met up with a very unusual Earth person. We don't all take our anger out on a punching bag."

Sixe, tactful by nature, replied with humor, "Still, Adam's friends taught me a great deal, Marc Aurèle. And the finest thing I learned was probably what is called friendship."

The green rays landed on the embarrassed face of Adam who seemed stiff and uncomfortable.

"I hope, Adam," said Commander Sixe very seriously, "that none of these revelations will change your attitude to your robot. No one must suspect the truth of my existence or the role of Cyber."

"No, Commander. Very well, Commander,"

replied the two boys willingly.

Now it was Alex Vimont's turn to speak. "So as not to give away our secret, keep calling the robot Cyber and speak to him as you did before. When other people are around, Sixe will do his part by using his electronic voice. Don't be shy about asking him to do chores, just as you did before. Nothing must seem to have changed between you."

"But it's a little embarrassing," objected Adam, scratching his head. "I don't want to bother the . . . the . . ."

"You're forgetting that I'm not inside Cyber. At the mere touch of a button I can make him lift an automobile. My metallic voice and the humming motor inside Cyber are only there to complete the picture that young Earth people have of a robot. Neither or them is necessary."

"But thanks to them," Adam pointed out, "Amandara was able to make robots for us exactly like the ones in our science-fiction stories."

Until supper, Sixe told the spellbound children all about his planet and his people. He described his solitary life in the spacecraft orbiting around the earth.

"My colleague, Tefla, is in another vehicle and masterminds Nootka, Eve Kevin's robot."

Then he warned them, "If it should ever

happen that Cyber fails to answer when you call him, you'll know that I'm busy somewhere else. Try again later. But right now I feel that I'm too inactive, so I find your calls entertaining."

The campers were grilling steaks over the fire.

"We're back in the age when people lived in caves," commented the astronaut who was really enjoying himself.

Marc handed bananas to everyone and added, "And for dessert, we're going even further back—to our first ancestors, the apes."

"Uncle Alex," Adam asked, "what will happen if the United Governments find out that you've disobeyed their orders?"

A sad look came over the pilot's determined face. "They'll find out sooner or later. Late enough, I hope, for our rescue mission to have succeeded. Then there'll be a court martial for Kevin and me, and our careers will be ruined. But that's certainly preferable to the destruction of civilization."

Because he didn't want to worry the children, the astronaut failed to point out that the unsuspecting Earth people were the most threatened of all. If the cosmonauts failed in their rescue attempts, Earth would be lost. The destructive star would obliterate everything in its path, and that would mean the end of the world. But an astronaut can't be fearful and pessimistic. Alex recovered his good humor and joked with Sixe to cheer the boys.

They spent the evening inside the tent. The amazing Cyber demonstrated another of his talents by heating the tent and providing light with beams from his silver body.

Alex taught the boys the complicated rules to the game of Fala, and Marc mastered it very quickly. Adam, who was less keen, had to make a terrific effort to interest himself in math. But he realized that this mathematical training would be absolutely essential if he wanted to pass the admission exams for space cadet school, which was the first step on the way to becoming an astronaut. Now that he'd discussed it with Eve, his secret confidante, Adam wasn't going to let his poor eyesight stand in the way of his most cherished plans.

The pilot and Sixe still had things to discuss. At ten o'clock Alex chased his guests off to bed. Adam produced a tiny oil lamp, a birthday present from Millie.

"Now we'll be real *coureurs des bois*," said Marc, delighted with the flickering light that produced dancing shadows on the walls of the tent and made it hard to read the latest Tintin comic book.

Unfortunately nylon tents are not made to

stand much heat. Adam happened to look up and pointed in horror at the sloping roof. A round hole was rapidly growing bigger. Marc quickly blew out the lamp.

"Whew! That was a close call. I read somewhere that synthetic material can catch fire in an instant."

"Roasted in the prime of life," joked Adam with a forced laugh.

Their flashlights, more modern but safer, showed the extent of the disaster: a hole as big as a fist in the lining of the roof.

"Unreal!" moaned Marc in despair. "My dad's going to kill me. It's a brand new tent."

Marc was so upset that he totally forgot his former enthusiasm for primitive lighting and snarled, "You and your lousy oil lamp!"

He sullenly turned his back and, in spite of his nasty humor, soon went to sleep. Adam felt terribly guilty. He lay there anxiously watching for Cyber who had promised to come and keep the tent warm during the night.

Adam thought of asking the robot's advice, but now he felt rather shy about bothering someone as important as a cosmonaut from Amandara with such small details.

When the robot glided into the tent, skilfully jumping over Zabulon who suspected nothing, Adam showed him the damage. Cyber stretched out his arm and touched the burnt fabric.

Using the sympathetic voice of Commander Six, he whispered, "I've studied your planet's chemistry a little. I have just analysed the composition of this nylon, and I think I can repair the damage if you can get me the necessary materials. I'll need Rilsan, or a by-product of euphorbiaceae."

"What the heck is that? I'll never find it."

"Earth people call it castor oil. You can get it in the shops where you buy your medicines."

"In the drugstore? That's the best yet! A tent made of castor oil!"

"Nylon synthesized by the polycondensation of amino-undecanoic acids," explained Six with the precision of a true scientist.

"I'll believe you," said Adam. Then, comforted by his space friend's knowledge and skill, he went off to sleep.

Cyber stood between the two sleeping bags. He raised a pincer above the head of each sleeping boy and shone a faint yellow beam over them.

In the morning the two boys were completely amazed to learn that, impossible as it seemed, they'd both had exactly the same dream.

They had been riding in a spaceship with a picture window that looked out on the vast starry sky. A planet gleamed in the distance. The now familiar voice of Sixe said, "See how beautiful your Earth looks from space."

The interior of the spaceship, all gentle curves and flowing lines, was entirely white. Its lighting seemed to come from a warm glow. The pilot's seat could be turned into a bed. It was surrounded by many instrument panels with hundreds of different colored lights.

Hanging from the ceiling and in every available space were all kinds of green plants that gave freshness and life to the cabin. The boys were rather surprised to see all this unexpected greenery amidst the impersonal machines. The cosmonaut smiled at their astonishment.

"Amandarians can't live without greenery. We always carry the symbols of our Green Planet with us. These plants give us pleasure, but they also provide air and food. Try some."

He picked several leaves and handed them to his guests. The boys were too embarrassed to refuse. Imitating their host, they cautiously tasted what he'd offered them. Later on when they compared notes, they both agreed that the plant had tasted delicious, like fresh mint.

The Amandarian in their dream, a splendid man dressed all in white, matched the descriptions the astronauts had given them: tall, handsome, with silver hair and green eyes. The boys were impressed by his dignified manner. Even though they were wildly curious, neither had the nerve to ask many questions in his own dream.

Commander Six had shown them a control panel and a small screen on which Adam and Marc were able to see themselves asleep in their sleeping bags. It was a three-dimensional picture showing every corner of the tent in detail, including the hole in the tent roof.

"This is what Cyber can see now, and what he shows me at the same time. My colleague Tefla and I were only supposed to be spectators and not do anything to interfere in your lives, but you've won our sympathy. Thanks to you both, and to little Eve in Vancouver, we've had some very pleasant times. Don't worry. This situation is only temporary. We have no intention of imposing on you like this for very long."

When the boys opened their eyes, sun was filtering through the orange roof of the tent. Cyber stood guard between them. Adam and Marc talked about the strange dream they'd each had. They looked at one another, feeling uneasy and trying to picture what their waking moments would look like on the tiny screen in the sky.

That morning the slaves of Round Lake took Alex to the deserted house. They stayed in their boat and looked at the house from a distance.

"The location is fine," Alex declared. "I'll sign the papers and the next time we come, we'll be the owners."

Marc didn't say anything, but as the son of a real estate agent, he found this careless way of buying a house somewhat surprising. It actually seemed as though Captain Vimont had chosen the site rather than the cottage. And the observant young neighbor was not mistaken.

According to the agreement reached a month earlier by Alex and Colonel Kevin, the first phase of Plan B had been put in place.

CHAPTER SIX

During the month of November, Alex Vimont bought the house on Round Lake and had some remodelling done. The whole family, and Marc as well, squeezed into the Capra Five and went to inspect the work and spend a memorable weekend.

Mr. Harel, who was always ready to lend a hand, let them borrow his camp-equipment trailer. They loaded it with an impressive array of gear: blankets, pots and pans, food, and even snowshoes, in case winter decided to pay a visit.

At the turn-off from the main road, the pilot stopped his car. He handed two keys to his nephew and pointed to a small windowless cabin that was almost hidden by trees.

"As you see, I've had a little shelter built over there for a snowmobile which I'll need to reach the cottage in winter. Would you go and put the snowshoes and this flashlight in it? Hang onto the keys. They're your own keys to this cabin and to the cottage."

Adam carefully placed the keys in his wallet. It pleased him when his uncle or his mother showed their confidence in him and gave him responsibilities.

Just as he was getting back into the car, a bus went noisily by, raising a cloud of dust.

The astronaut explained, "We've even got transportation at our door. The Saint-Jovite bus goes by here every day. If Adam and Marc ever want to come up here by themselves, it's only a five-kilometre walk to the cottage."

"Is five kilometres very far?" asked Millie who was wriggling with impatience.

The bumpy road that led to the lake wound through the fir trees. The low branches brushed the silver roof of the Capra and its bouncing trailer. Marc took this opportunity to boast, "Five kilometres? That's peanuts for *coureurs des bois* like us. We'd be hardly out of breath when we got there. Right, Adam?"

"If you're going to be out of breath, why run at all?" asked Millie who was not easily impressed.

Another surprise was waiting for them on the shore of the lake. Alex Vimont had bought a flat-bottomed boat with a small, sluggish motor.

The slaves of Round Lake were put in charge of unloading and moving in. Even with the robot's help, it took three trips before they managed to get all the passengers and their baggage into the renovated cottage.

It was dark by the time Adam and Marc unloaded the last case of canned food. Although they knew that the mother bear and all the other bears were hibernating, the boys hurried up the well-worn path. Zabulon leaped happily beside them, and the watchful Cyber brought up the rear.

The shutters were open, and through the windows came the comforting glow of oil lamps. Marc and Adam completed their chores by carrying in armfuls of logs from the stand of trees beside the cottage. Then, famished and feeling pleased with themselves, they went inside to wash in the icy water from the pump.

The furniture was rustic and comfortable. A good fire crackled in the grate. Millie and her mother had unrolled the sleeping bags and spread the blankets on the bunk beds.

An iron kettle simmered on the wood stove and from it came the irresistible aroma of baked beans for which Uncle Alex was famous.

The two-day holiday was pleasant and peaceful. In the evening Adam and Marc took on Cyber and the astronaut in a game of Fala.

With each game they played, the rules became more complicated, demanding more and more calculations. But thanks to coaching from Eve and his robot, Adam could now enjoy this sort of exercise which would be part of his life if he were to become a space pilot.

As soon as they returned on Monday evening, Adam, with Cyber's cooperation, rushed to tell his friend in Vancouver all about his weekend. Much to his surprise, the little girl told him about a similar expedition with the colonel and her Aunt Corinne.

"Daddy bought a cottage in the mountains too, far away from any other houses. We've got a wonderful view of the whole valley. Daddy says it's 'my' cottage, and I've got the key on a chain around my neck."

"Mine's in my pocket."

At the time, the coincidence of having almost the same experience didn't occur to the children. They were too carried away by their excitement.

"Marc and I went all around the lake in our boat. Millie went head first overboard and was screaming in six inches of freezing water. Cyber fished her out and warmed her up. We found a beaver dam and Zabulon got hit on the nose by one of the beaver's tails. What happened to you, Eve?"

"I scaled Black Mountain with Aunt Corinne

who's crazy about mountain climbing. And I climbed all the fir trees around the place. Nootka was really surprised. On Amandara the trees don't have low branches, so she'd never seen anybody do that. I told her it's because we're descended from monkeys, and she believed me—till she looked it up in her data bank. We had a good laugh about that."

Adam envied her boldness. He wouldn't dream of being so cheeky to Sixe. While Eve and her robot had become closer since she'd met Tefla, the constant presence of Sixe had come more and more between Adam and his old pal Cyber.

As he did every Monday, Adam asked, "Do you want me to help you with your French homework?"

"No thanks, Adam. Now that I know your language better, the sentences are a lot easier. Do you want to play Fala? Daddy taught me a new problem."

"And I've got some new answers. Wait till I set it up. Okay. Are you ready?"

At each end of the country, in the soft glow coming from the robots that faced them, two children sprawled on their stomachs in front of their Amandarian game. The hour went by quickly and they said goodnight, very pleased with each other. Their friendship and their means of communicating must surely have been the most unique in the world.

But if Eve and Adam were happy, Earth, on the other hand, was beginning to undergo strange and disastrous hardships. Tidal waves, earthquakes, and power failures struck one continent after another, causing more and more frequent catastrophes. There seemed to be no earthly explanation. Scientists concluded that they were the result of atmospheric conditions and mysterious forces in space.

During the month of December, the power failures increased. Sometimes they lasted for several days, plaguing the entire country with problems of communication, heating, lighting, and running water.

At first, most children, whether they were in Montreal or in Vancouver, thought it was fun to have makeshift suppers by candlelight. They liked the closed schools and the picnics with family or friends who were lucky enough to have fireplaces to heat their freezing houses. Soon, however, wood was rationed; there was a shortage of candles; tins of food were impossible to find, and there was no fresh produce at all.

When the power returned in one country, the radio and television would report similar calamities in other places. Life was disturbed all over the planet, and each country struggled for survival.

Marc had to stay with the Colberts when his parents were away from home during the blackouts. Mrs. Harel was a nurse and she spent her days and nights with those who were sick. The generators could only provide essential services to hospitals. More and more people would probably die from the cold and from accidents. Mr. Harel who had joined the civil defence brigade, was also away for long spells, helping to keep order in the now imperilled city.

Mireille Colbert was glad to take in the young neighbor. She often had to go with Millie to comfort her invalid mother who lived in Three Rivers. Adam and Marc stayed alone together, but Mireille felt that they were safe under Cyber's protection. With light and heat from the robot, the boys were more comfortable than most other people on the globe.

Eve and her aunt also enjoyed Nootka's protection. The warmer climate in British Columbia meant that there were fewer hardships, but lack of running water, no telephones, and closed stores complicated their daily life.

From time to time the earth would heave. The tremors could be felt from one ocean to the other, though fortunately they were not too violent. It was much worse in Europe and Asia.

But the most terrible thing for everyone was

the mystery of these unexplained events, the uncertain future, and a growing panic among the people because, sometimes for weeks on end, there were no newspapers, no radio, and no television. What was happening in the rest of the world?

Just when their families needed them most, the astronauts were called up by the Air Ministry and had to be away more than ever. They spent weeks at a time in underground bases that had been built in isolated parts of the country. Hidden under six hundred feet of concrete, complicated equipment analysed reports sent from lunar headquarters, from satellites, and from detection devices in every country on Earth.

Little by little one conclusion seemed unavoidable. Earth was the target of an attack from another planet. But in order to avoid a panic, the United Governments delayed revealing the disastrous news.

Christmas day in this year of hardship went by almost unnoticed in an America plunged into darkness. Mireille was once again at Three Rivers with Millie. Torn between duties, she had to leave her eldest child in Cyber's care and with Marc Harel who was also alone.

Adam and the robot were under strict orders

from Alex Vimont not to go far from the city unless expressly told to do so. Eve and Nootka were under the same restrictions. Like soldiers in wartime, the astronauts' families obeyed blindly, resigning themselves to the inevitable and waiting for instructions.

On that December 25, Adam and Marc were together alongside the robot who kept them warm and gave them light as best it could. Outside a storm was raging, and the snow swirled in howling gusts through the dark deserted streets.

"It's not what you'd call a great Christmas," Adam lamented as he chewed his sandwich of dry bread.

"Well, say what you like," replied Marc with his mouth full, "you can't beat ketchup for changing the taste of our eternal peanut butter—even though you thought it was gross when I first suggested it. I was right about it after all."

"Yeah, but it's not like a turkey dinner with Christmas cake. Or family gatherings."

"Listen here, chum, if it weren't for Cyber, we'd be spending the week packed in with my Aunt Alice and her gang of whining brats. It's ultra-incredible how lucky we are to have that robot."

"You're right."

Adam was sorry he'd been so ungrateful. He stretched out on the red sofa with Zabulon at his feet and commanded, "Cyber, take our minds off all this. Pretend you're a Christmas tree and give us a concert."

The robot extended its arms. Rays of all colors sparkled here and there in the joints of his framework. Then, like a stereo cassette player, he played Christmas carols that he'd heard during the occasional times when the radios were still working. Lost in their dream of Christmas, the boys listened in silence to memories of holiday seasons.

"Silent night, holy night, . . ."

Suddenly Marc jumped up and cried in husky voice, "Enough! You'll have me bawling in a minute. Adam, let's talk to your English friend with the nice voice instead. I love her accent and her jokes."

Adam had been forced to introduce his two friends to each other, and was now a bit jealous noticing how well they got along. Marc was very self-confident and liked to show off.

"I'm crazy about redheads," he cooed like a real lady-killer.

"Your accent is very . . . interesting," replied Eve who was never at a loss for words.

The three children consoled themselves by exchanging Christmas greetings, recipes that needed no cooking, and bilingual jokes that lost a good deal in the translation. They played Fala and tried to outdo each other with new ideas. Eve and Marc were better at math, but Adam could think up devilish strategies.

Marc had just finished a mental calculation and changed the rings from one peg to another. He was about to start his next play when all at once he interrupted himself to exclaim, "Unrealest of the unreal! I just thought of something. We've got the only means of communication in the whole world! Even the short waves are jammed."

From the mouth of Cyber, a sad little voice answered. "It's true. And we're using it for dumb things like gabbing and playing games. Couldn't we do something useful with our robots?"

"No," said Adam firmly. "Uncle Alex made a point of telling me that the robots are useful because nobody knows what they can do. If the United Governments suspected, they'd destroy them. We've got our orders. Let's just wait."

Marc wasn't sure whether he ought to admire these childish junior officers or make fun of them.

"Incredible! You're not in the army, you know."

"Maybe not," replied Eve, "but even though the rest of the world doesn't know it, we're at war.

Daddy said so."

If Adam had been by himself, Eve might have confided her worries to him. She might perhaps have dared to admit that she was afraid of the dark, of the violent weather, and the scary future. But in front of Marc the show-off who wasn't as sensitive as her friend, Eve hid her feelings and acted like a heroine. What she didn't know was that the two bewildered boys were inspired by her example and didn't want to admit their fears to a girl as brave as she seemed.

By New Year's Day the electricity was back on in Canada, but then hurricanes and raging winds began to sweep the planet. Gradually life returned to normal, the schools reopened, and the United Governments, having learned from experience, were better prepared from one alert to the next.

Even though calm had been restored, the two astronauts didn't come home to their families. Without ever saying so openly, their superiors suspected them of knowing more than they let on. Their every move was carefully watched. They'd been given strict orders not to leave the underground base at North Bay, Ontario.

"They're handling us with kid gloves," Alex confided to Kevin when they managed to meet in the base cafeteria. "But we're actually under arrest."

"You're right. They listen in on our phone calls and read our mail."

"I was ordered to warn Mireille that from today on, the house will be under twenty-four-hour surveillance by security agents of the United Governments. My sister was furious."

"I had to give the same message to my sister. But she, on the contrary, was delighted to have their protection. She's always been afraid that some nut will blame all our problems on the robots and take it out on Eve."

Six days later, the astronomers in the observatories noted the presence of a mysterious star that seemed to be headed towards Earth. At the same time the lunar base spotted suspicious spacecraft. Further investigation confirmed that they were Amandarian rocket ships. This invasion worried the Earth people much more than the passing of a distant meteor whose power they still couldn't estimate.

"WE ARE THREATENED BY THE AMANDAR-IAN FLEET," screamed the headlines of the world's newspapers.

Immediately the governments and everyone who had been against helping the Green Planet triumphed. Now they could identify their enemy.

Dislike and mistrust of the two astronauts

grew, and the security net tightened around their families. Alex Vimont and David Kevin were held prisoner, forbidden to leave the underground headquarters. They managed, through great ingenuity, to meet each other in the boiler room. The roar of the machines prevented the wire-taps from recording their conversation.

Alex whispered, "This is war, Kevin. And we've become the enemy. You know what that means?"

The colonel nodded his head. "Yes. We'll have to abandon Plan B. I thought we'd have more time. There's nothing left now but the final possibility—and that hasn't been perfected yet."

"Plan C! I was hoping we wouldn't have to get the children mixed up in it. They aren't ready for it."

"They're pretty smart, Alex. They'll do what's necessary. And our sisters will help them. We've got to warn them. But how? We're forbidden to communicate with the outside world."

"There's only one way," said Alex. "If we use it, they'll throw us into prison for sure, but it's all we've got. Our kids will have to act very fast. The authorities will pounce on the robots and destroy them instantly."

The two pilots had only a few minutes to make their plans because some officers who suspected them soon came along and kept a constant watch on them. That same night they separated the two astronauts by sending Kevin to another underground base on the Alaska border.

Held captive and cut off from the outside world, the only two men who could save Earth were now powerless. The fate of the planet rested on the shoulders of two children who were sleeping peacefully, totally unaware of the task that lay ahead of them.

"You're a good guy to help me with my papers, Marc. That Mr. Jerome absolutely refuses to let Cyber out of the house."

"That's because he likes to play chess with him. And 'cause a government agent thinks it's fun to have a robot serve him his coffee."

The young neighbor who was pulling the sled with the box of newspapers on it, didn't mind showing his resentment. He was still staying with the Colberts because Adam's mother and sister hadn't come back from Three Rivers. Adam's grandmother had broken her ankle during the last blackout and Mireille had to stay with her until she was well enough to be moved.

It was bitterly cold and the shivering Marc was not exactly thrilled at having to work outdoors while the agent who was supposed to be protecting the Colberts lounged around in the warm house and monopolized the helpful robot.

"No, that's not why," protested Adam who really liked Mr. Jerome. "He's got his orders and besides, this is the time when he has to phone in his report to his boss."

"Unbelievable! Who the heck cares? With all your new customers, it's also the time when you really need Cyber."

"You're almost as fast as he is, even if you're not as strong," said Adam who was more grateful than he was tactful. "But the paper isn't very heavy. I feel as if I'm cheating my customers by only giving them four little pages."

"You're not the one who prints it. Everybody knows paper is scarce and they're rationing it like everything else."

"Anyway, with all the breakdowns in communication, there's not very much news to write."

The boys stopped in front of a big four-storey building. A lot of customers lived there. They divided up the skimpy copies of the paper into two large canvas bags that were marked with the name *La Presse*.

Adam spurred himself on by saying, "Still, *La Presse* is pretty valuable now that we can't depend on the radio and the TV. It makes me feel useful. Do you want to take the two lower floors? I'll take the upper ones."

"You're hoping to get some candy from that

old lady, eh?"

"Mainly I go there to cheer her up and do errands for her. My mom asked me to invite her to our place if the blackouts start again."

"With me, and your grandmother from Three Rivers, and Mr. Jerome, it'll be a real circus in there!"

His bag over his shoulder, Marc turned and pointed his mitten at a car that had been following them ever since they'd left their house. It was stopped by the curb now, waiting.

"There's another one who's not killing himself with work—sitting in a warm car all day long. His boss told him, 'Follow that dangerous enemy Adam Colbert and his sinister accomplice Marc Harel. Never let them out of your sight.' And I thought secret agents led an exciting life!"

Adam merely said, "It must be pretty boring most of the time."

He was always hoping kidnappers or muggers would appear and he'd be involved in a tremendous battle. Naturally he'd play the starring role, with some minor assistance from Marc.

After waving to Mr. Hébert, their patient escort, the boys rushed into the building. They'd be inside for at least twenty minutes, and the agent took the opportunity to open a copy of the newspaper that Adam, who was a good kid, had offered him.

There were stories about ordeals in Australia, China, and India. It was now their turn to be rocked by disasters, just as America and Europe were barely recovering from their troubles. One whole page contained a list of supplies to stock up on before the next alert, because no one doubted that there would be more calamities to come.

There was an announcement in huge letters about a program planned for that evening. Canadian representatives from the United Governments were going to make some very serious statements. The entire population was asked to listen to the discussion which would be heard at the same time on both the French and the English networks.

In addition, the leaders of every country in the world would be presenting similar programs, provided that there was electricity that day.

They were going to analyse Earth's situation. Several experts would offer their opinions; astronomers would study the path of the travelling meteor; seismologists would talk about the earthquakes; meteorologists would discuss the upheavals in the weather. Engineers and doctors would give opinions, and finally, the two astronauts who were well-known experts on the subject of Amandara Tetra, Colonel David Kevin and Captain Alexandre Vimont, would speak.

CHAPTER SEVEN

Both boys were settled on the red sofa in their pajamas, next to Mr. Jerome. An attentive Cyber and an indifferent Zabulon were also listening to the speeches by Canada's representatives of the United Governments of the Earth.

The program was being broadcast from the underground headquarters where Canada's leaders and the chiefs of her armed forces had gathered. Because of the extreme urgency of the world situation, two programs were being shown simultaneously, one in English and one in French. Rooms had been set up on either side of the main studio. The speakers went from one room to the other so that the whole country, from the Atlantic to the Pacific, could learn at the same time what these leaders had to say.

The news was bad; in fact, it was terrifying.

Spaceships of unknown origin were ploughing through space. The detection devices at the lunar base couldn't identify them.

Worse still, a travelling star seemed to be heading towards Earth. It was so massive that it was upsetting the atmosphere, and its speed created waves that interfered with the sources of energy. That's what had caused the power failures.

There was a grave risk that the planet would be completely destroyed if this star continued on its present path.

Two small satellites orbiting the planet were the only things that could be positively identified. They belonged to Amandara Tetra. Piloted by Tefla and Sixe, they represented an unspecified danger. Were they merely observation stations, or were they outposts for a murderous cosmic fleet? Was the ominous star really controlled by extra-terrestrial beings?

For the first time, the planet Earth was being told the whole truth. After months of uncertainty, people in every nation were informed about the dangers looming over them. One by one the experts candidly set out the risks.

No commercials interrupted this broadcast, the most tragic and realistic one the screen had ever shown. Families, gathered together to comfort each other, listened gravely.

It was ten o'clock before the camera focussed on the two impressive-looking astronauts in their silver high-collared uniforms. Across their chests were the black and gold lightning flashes of the space fleet's insignia. Both men gave the traditional salute of rocket ship pilots, a raised fist with the thumb pointing to the sky.

David Kevin looked pale and worried; his colleague wore his usual happy-go-lucky expression and his wry smile. Alex Vimont was preparing to gamble with his future as casually as he had so often gambled with his life during interplanetary flights.

The two were still popular heroes. People just couldn't help admiring these fearless astronauts. The public didn't know that these same men were under suspicion, that they were in disfavor, and that armed guards were watching their every move.

The United Governments, aware that the audience wanted to see the astronauts, didn't dare prevent them from appearing. But they kept a close eye on them. Their speeches had been studied and approved. Although the pilots wouldn't be able to say everything that was on their minds, they'd be able to reassure the public.

The English camera focussed on Colonel Kevin while the French networks showed the man from Quebec, whose green eyes and straight fair hair were as familiar as the faces of television's most famous stars.

Both astronauts recalled the help they'd been given on Amandara. Then they stressed the Amandarians' knowledge, their great wisdom, and their humanity. The quiet assurance of their words calmed the audience who sensed a growing menace hanging over the world.

"We are firmly convinced that no cosmic power is attacking our planet directly. The misfortunes that have struck Earth are the result of wars that have nothing to do with us. That doesn't make the catastrophes less severe, but at least we have a chance of surviving. Because if one of these powers really wanted to destroy our world, there'd be nothing we could do about it.

"Let's hope these battles move away from our solar system and that Earth will escape from this nightmare unharmed. Be confident that we have the support and the sympathy of the Amandarians. As my friend Sixe from the Green Planet, said . . ."

With a mischievous smile Alex Vimont reeled off a few sentences in the mysterious dialect of Amandara Tetra. The syllables were strung together musically, as if to prove to the world that a people who spoke such a harmonious language could never be violent and destructive.

The astronaut was supposed to have talked longer, but his image was suddenly erased from the screen. The calm face of Mrs. Petry, one of the most prominent Canadians in the United Governments, appeared instead. Without commenting on the abrupt disappearance of the astronauts, she urged the public to be calm and disciplined.

"We expect there will be further alarms soon. Our equipment is now able to detect, but not avert them. Be brave. Have faith in the future. Pray. Help one another. Be prepared, and follow the instructions given by the security officers. May peace be with you."

The program was over. At the underground headquarters, Mrs. Petry and her three colleagues spoke briefly with each other and then turned to the two astronauts, standing motionless under the threat of guns trained on them.

Mrs. Petry pointed to the astronauts. "These two officers have communicated with the enemy. The phrases they spoke in Amandarian grossly exceeded the greetings we authorized. They are traitors. They must be placed under arrest and court-martialled as quickly as possible.

"Colonel Kevin, Captain Vimont, you were once heroes, but you know the penalty for treason in time of war if you are found guilty."

David and Alex exchanged triumphant glances and gave each other a slight farewell wave. Without protest they followed the guards. The doors of their cells clanged shut. The wait, which they would spend in hope and anxiety, had begun.

It was quite possible that they would be condemned to death. But their message had been sent. Others would now continue the battle.

When the program ended, the boys, along with Cyber and Zabulon, went down to Adam's basement room to get ready for bed.

Mr. Jerome checked all the doors and windows in the house. He spread blankets out on the red sofa where he slept each night.

Marc was loaded down with his usual nightly provisions of dried apples and cookies. Cyber carried glasses and a litre of powdered milk. As Marc handed out the snack, he began to talk excitedly about the television program they'd just seen.

"Unbelievable! We're not out of the woods yet. More blackouts and storms! I'll have to keep sleeping on this bearskin of yours. Here, have some of this. You might as well enjoy it before we have to go back to eating nothing but peanut butter again."

Just then Marc noticed how quiet and pale his

friend was. Worried, he went over to Adam who was sitting, stunned, at the foot of his bed.

"What's the matter with you? You're as white as a sheet. Your eyes look all red. Hey, pal, is something wrong? Did it upset you to see your uncle? I think he was the most optimistic of the whole gang."

"He spoke to me," whispered Adam, giving his friend a dazed look. "He spoke to me."

"Of course he spoke to you. He spoke to me too, and to millions of other people. That's what he was there for. Unreal! Come on."

"No, Marc. He spoke to me in Amandarian . . . and I understood him. I understood his message. He said . . ."

"You mean you can speak that Green Planet lingo? Since when?"

"I . . . I don't know. But Uncle Alex was talking to me. Just to me and nobody else. And I understood."

"That's the weirdest thing I ever heard! So, what did your uncle say?"

Adam looked his friend in the eye and lowered his voice, very conscious of how serious the message was.

"He said, 'Son of my sister . . .'"

"Isn't that kind of formal for your Uncle Alex?"

"There's no word in Amandarian for nephew."

And then Adam quickly interrupted himself to say, "Hey, how did I know that? Anyway, Uncle Alex said to me, 'Son of my sister, it's up to you to do something. You will save the world. You will follow the third plan. Do exactly as Sixe tells you. He will guide you. Go to Round Lake and . . .' "

"And what?" asked Marc who was crouched on the floor by the bed.

One look at Adam's solemn face and quivering lip convinced Marc that he was serious. Adam seemed lost in a daydream, so Marc shook him and insisted, "Then what did he say?"

Adam came back to earth. He explained, "My uncle was interrupted. The picture disappeared. He didn't finish his message."

"I bet they thought he was gabbing too much in the enemy's language," said Marc, hitting the nail on the head.

"I don't know what to do, Marc. I'll never be able to do it. Uncle Alex is counting on me and I don't know what to do. I don't know anything about the third plan. I don't even know the first one."

Tears of discouragement ran down the boy's pale cheeks. He took off his glasses and impatiently wiped his eyes with the back of his hand.

But Marc never ceased to be practical. He

said, "Don't lose your cool. Your uncle said Sixe would guide you. Hey, Cyber. What're you waiting for?"

The robot came over to them. He answered in his meek voice, "I was wait-ing for or-ders, mas-ter."

Adam smiled through his tears. If Sixe was still able to tease him, all was not lost.

Humbly, the master asked his robot, "What should I do?"

Marc interrupted, sounding suspicious. "First of all, how come Adam can speak Amandarian when he never learned it?"

"Marc Aurèle," said the voice of Sixe very solemnly, "you have a talent for asking pertinent questions. I taught Adam my language while he slept, just as Tefla taught it to Eve Kevin. We were preparing you in case Colonel Kevin and Captain Vimont would not be available at the crucial moment. That moment has arrived, and our friends are no longer able to help us. It's up to you."

In a thin faltering voice, Adam said, "I don't know very much, but Uncle Alex said I could help you. Tell me what to do and I'll obey you. Marc will do his part too. Right, Marc?"

"Hey, you don't have to ask. Of course I'll help Adam — he's my friend."

The neighbor may have lacked Adam's

overwhelming enthusiasm for the Green Planet's cause, but he had very clear ideas about what friendship should be.

The robot stretched out its arm and touched both boys on the shoulder. Sixe's voice sounded warm and emotional. "You are brave children. Your names will go down in the history of my people."

"Will they build a monument to us?" joked Marc who was a bit hopeful that Sixe might say yes.

But Adam was so absorbed in his new responsibilities that he broke up this polite little exchange.

He came straight to the point. "Sixe, do you know what the third plan is? Uncle Alex mentioned Round Lake. What are we supposed to do?"

To the boys' great surprise, Cyber answered by beginning to recite a page from "Souvenirs" by Arthur Conan Doyle! The robot had recently read this story to Adam. As he recited the passage, he put his pincer up to his grille in a clumsy way, giving a comical imitation of someone asking for silence. Then he pointed to the stairs.

The padded door opened slightly, without making a sound. Mr. Jerome heard the robot's monotonous voice reading in an even tone:

"Sherlock Holmes gave a small laugh. 'My dear Watson, I have the advantage of knowing your habits. When your visits to the sick are brief, you make them on foot. When they are long, you take a cab. Today, your shoes are not dusty. I deduce from this that your day has been sufficiently busy to justify the cab.'

" 'Bravo,' I exclaimed."

" 'It's elementary,' he said."

Mr. Jerome was relieved. He thought he'd heard a man's voice. The world situation had made him very tense. He interrupted the story to call from the landing, "Is everything all right, kids?"

"Yes, Mr. Jerome. Cyber's just finishing the story. There's only one more chapter left, and then we'll turn out the light."

Adam wasn't very good at telling a lie with a sincere voice. He also knew that Mr. Jerome felt burdened with the responsibilities of looking after the children in place of Adam's mother. Mr. Jerome's line of work and his bachelor's life hadn't prepared him for it. All the agent could think to do was repeat vaguely the advice his own mother had always given him—forgetting that he'd seldom followed it.

"Don't stay up too late."

The door closed again. Without making a sound, Mr. Jerome piled up some tin cans outside the door and put a bell on the top. No one could get by there without sounding the alarm. However it wasn't from two youngsters, an overfriendly dog, and a toy robot that an attack could be expected.

Any danger would more likely come from outside. But watchful fellow agents were in a parked car out front, and others were patrolling the neighborhood. Mr. Jerome went to sleep feeling safe. He was totally unaware of the plot that was brewing in the darkness, and of the urgent whispering underneath the very room where he slept so peacefully.

It was only six o'clock in the evening when Canada's west coast tuned in to hear the message from the United Governments.

When her father spoke directly to her in Amandarian, Eve felt the same emotions that her friend in Quebec had experienced. She was sure that the colonel had looked straight into her eyes while the personal message implanted itself in her memory:

"My little daughter, I am a prisoner here. You will have to take my place. Have complete faith in Tefla and my sister. We are moving to Plan C.

You must go . . ."

"He didn't tell me where to go!" cried Eve all upset. She turned to her aunt, "Daddy didn't finish his sentence. Oh! Aunt Corinne, what are we going to do?"

"Did you understand the message in Amandarian?" asked the astonished Corinne who knew nothing about the robot's language lessons in the middle of the night. Like Alex, David Kevin had been hoping they'd never get to the third plan, Plan C.

Aunt Corinne wasn't the type to make a fuss over complications or to indulge in pointless emotions. She went straight to the heart of the problem.

"Calm yourself, my pet. You're all worked up. What did your father say?"

Eve repeated the message. Then Tefla broke in.

"I know what you have to do, Eve. I'll guide you, and you will help me."

Suddenly the physicist remembered her brother's directions.

"I got some instructions from David too. At the time I didn't pay much attention, but I think I can remember. Sometimes I'm a bit absent-minded," she added quite unnecessarily. She turned to the robot.

"If I understood correctly, you and Eve must

go to that remote cottage at Black Mountain, several hours before the next alert. Is that right?"

"Ex-ac-tly," replied the robot. "Plan C. Mess-age un-der-stood."

"That doesn't seem very complicated," said Eve's aunt. "On the television they predicted a power failure for tomorrow night. I've got an important meeting at the university at noon. As soon as it's over, I'll come back here. You can jump in my car and we'll head for the cottage. We'll be there by supper time. There's nothing difficult about that. And the blackout won't bother us because there's no electricity up there anyway."

"But Aunt Corinne, what'll we do about the agents who are supposed to be protecting us? They're sitting out there in their car right in front of the house. They follow us everywhere we go. Today they even drove me home from school."

The physicist had overlooked these details. With a very determined air, she announced in her most confident voice, "I can manage to lose anybody who dares to chase me on the highway. They do it in all the police shows on television. All you have to do is to apply a few rules from physics."

Eve found it hard to imagine her aunt's Volkswagen transformed into a racing car, but she'd also seen lots of films in which the good people always triumphed. She raised a second objection.

"That agent out in the hall always wants to know where I'm going when I leave. He watches the elevator."

"You can tell him you're going to your piano lesson. Carry your music case with you."

Obviously Aunt Corinne hadn't wasted her time while watching her favorite police shows. She could dream up first-rate plots.

Then her niece spelled out the third difficulty, the most serious one. "The agents will never let Nootka leave the apartment."

But the robot itself solved this impossible problem. "I can go out on the balcony and meet you in the lane behind the building. I'll jump down from the third floor."

"You'll get smashed to smithereens in the fall!" cried Eve horrified.

"I can float. You saw me do it when I climbed the stairs."

To show what she meant, Nootka silently lifted off and hovered near the ceiling.

"Good. We're all set then," said Aunt Corinne. All these little problems were keeping her from her work. Ever since the mysterious discovery of the plus sign in her formulas, the abnormality in the magnetic momentum seemed to be almost at her fingertips.

"I'll pack our suitcases this evening. The supplies are already at the cottage. Your father suspected that we might have to leave on the spur of the moment. He always plans ahead."

Eve smiled indulgently at the robot. Her aunt had already forgotten that the colonel himself had drawn up Plan C and that he'd bought the cottage at Black Mountain for just this situation.

When she was alone in her room, Eve wondered if she ought to contact Adam, as she did every night. She was dying to ask him if he too, had received a message in Amandarian. But she held off because she knew that at the Colbert's Marc and Mr. Jerome were always around. Her friend didn't have many chances to be alone with Cyber. And maybe Adam's neighbor wasn't in on *all* the mysteries of the robots.

Weighed down by her enormous secret, Eve worried about her own part in this adventure. Her father had said that he was a prisoner. How could he be a prisoner when he was a famous hero and appeared on television? And how was she able to understand the language of the Green Planet without ever studying it, when she still had trouble with French despite Adam's help and her own efforts?

The robot approached the bed and stroked

Eve's red hair. This was now a familiar gesture. Tefla's enchanting voice explained, reassured, and soothed the little girl until she fell asleep feeling confident, in spite of what lay ahead for the next day.

It was five o'clock and darkness was falling as Adam and Marc filled their bags with copies of *La Presse*. After giving their constant escort a friendly wave, they rushed into the apartment building where Mrs. Babin lived. The car had picked them up at school, taken them home, waited at the door for them, and followed them while they delivered their papers. Mr. Hébert, the agent, looked at his watch, logged the time in his notebook, and then devoted himself to reading the four-page *La Presse*. It would be twenty or thirty minutes before his "charges" emerged from the building.

On this day, though, the two boys had other plans. They took the stairs down to the deserted basement and left their newspaper bags behind some garbage cans. Adam felt guilty because his subscribers had paid for those papers.

"Hurry up! We've got to get changed," puffed Marc as he pulled off his shabby suede coat. Underneath it he wore his orange ski parka.

Adam stuffed his leather jacket and Marc's coat in the janitor's broom closet. He put on a white tuque with a pompom. In his blue ski jacket and the tuque, Adam looked entirely different. Their hearts thumping, the two accomplices crept to the service door at the rear of the building. They opened it a crack and looked out into the lane. Nobody was there.

Running in the shadows of the buildings, the fugitives slipped between two garages, climbed a fence, and came out on the next street. Walking quickly, but not running because they didn't dare make themselves look suspicious, Adam and Marc disappeared into the subway station.

"Phew!" gasped Adam as he slumped into his seat. "Unseen and unrecognized. Let's hope Cyber gets away as easily."

"We're almost out of the woods. Have you got money for the bus tickets?"

Adam tapped his pocket. "Right here. Now I know why Uncle Alex gave me twenty dollars, in case . . . " His glasses had misted over, hiding his anxious expression.

"Do you think Cyber will be able to escape?" Adam repeated.

"Don't worry about that little tin man. He can always paralyse Jerome, if things go wrong."

Adam hadn't even thought of this disturbing alternative because the agent had always been so pleasant with the boys. Just how far would Cyber, or Sixe, go to succeed in his mission?

140

They'd have to trust Uncle Alex. The Amandarians were peaceful people. And yet Sixe had sworn that the robot would be waiting for them at the cottage on Round Lake when they arrived.

CHAPTER EIGHT

Mr. Jerome, his chin in his hands, sat staring in deep concentration at the chessboard. This evening he thought he had a chance of beating the crafty robot. The telephone interrupted his thinking. Six o'clock. The boss was calling for his nightly report.

Just as he did every evening, Cyber took this opportunity to glide out to the kitchen to feed the dog and make a cup of tea for the agent who took great pleasure in these little favors. Then he could brag afterward to his colleagues that he was "on a very special case" and had a robot to wait on him.

His message was brief: "Nothing to report." But Jerome had to write down a lot of instructions for the days to come, in case the power failure that had been predicted cut off all communications. The phone call went on and on.

The back door opened and closed. Zabulon could be heard barking in the yard. Mr. Jerome was pleased that the robot had let the dog out. But, contrary to his usual practice, Cyber had slipped out too, leaving the door ajar behind him. That way his friend Zabulon would be able to get back into the house. Cyber figured that no one would likely remember to let the dog in during the hue and cry that would follow the discovery of the strange disappearance of the robot and the children.

Soundlessly, Cyber rose straight up in the air until his little silver body was higher than the house. Then, with incredible speed, the robot gained altitude and sped away towards the north of Montreal. With great foresight, Alex Vimont had placed all the particulars of the location in Cyber's electronic memory. He was aimed in a straight line for Round Lake.

The robot landed softly on the veranda of the log cabin. A mountain of snow blocked the only door to the house. Cyber stretched out his pincers which began to emit burning rays. The snow melted and the doorway was clear.

Stationing himself in front of the door, the robot stood perfectly still and waited. His futuristic figure contrasted sharply with the rustic surroundings. In a few hours his sensors would pick up the approach of the two earthlings, Adam Colbert and Marc Harel.

Then the real work would begin, the mission for which Cyber had been designed, built, and sent to this inhospitable planet where the leaders had refused to help the endangered Amandara Tetra.

At seven o'clock the robot observed that, just as his detectors had foreseen, the power went off. The disaster was worldwide. Everywhere—on every point of the globe—the power stations had broken down simultaneously.

A few minutes earlier lunar headquarters had sent its last message to the underground shelters where the leaders of the threatened planet had taken refuge.

"It is now clear that the Worlaks, not the Amandarians, are responsible for this. Their space fleet, travelling on its vengeful path towards Amandara Tetra, will soon surround all sides of the globe. It was the Worlaks who aimed the star at us, the one that is causing all our hardships. This star will completely destroy the earth's atmosphere. It means the end of the world for human beings."

It was too late now to say "You were right" to the two astronauts locked in their cells. It was already too late even to warn the populations of the world.

It was too late for Earth!

"This cold is un-be-lievable! My hands are so numb they feel like a pair of boxing gloves. Are you sure this road's got an end to it?"

"Yes. My uncle said it was only five kilometres to the lake from the little cabin where the bus let us off."

"*Only* five kilometres! It's easy to see that your uncle never had to do his little five kilometres on snowshoes, at night, when it was colder than Greenland."

Marc clapped his hands to warm them up. Then, in a surly voice, he added, "It's too bad your uncle didn't get around to buying his snowmobile. Hand me your flashlight. It's my turn to light the way. Do you think the police'll come after us? Frankly, I wouldn't exactly hate being in jail right now."

"No. My uncle told me that he bought the cottage under a false name, to throw off the journalists. Nobody can trace us to this place."

"What about the bus driver?"

"Did you see the way everybody was racing to get home after the blackout? Nobody pays attention to other people at times like this."

"So, if we drop from exhaustion or hunger, we've had it, eh?"

Marc suddenly felt the weight of the darkness and the lonely wilderness that surrounded them. Though he'd been the one to encourage his less robust companion when they set out, he now felt his courage dissolving by the minute. A sharp crackling sound in the dark, close to the path, made them stop, paralysed with fear. They listened with total concentration. Nervously Marc swept the feeble rays of the flashlight over the bushes.

He whispered, "It's a bear!"

"No it's not. Listen! It's the cold making the branches snap. The bears are hibernating. They're asleep under the snow."

"Darn lucky for them," Marc muttered as he set off again in a hurry.

A mournful wailing came from the woods. It grew louder and louder. They stopped again, their hearts pounding.

"I hear wolves," whined Marc, shaking in his boots.

Adam, who wasn't much more confident than Marc, did his best to explain the scary sounds.

"It's the wind whipping between the two mountains. Wolves don't attack people—not unless they're starving."

"Who says they aren't?" complained his friend.

Adam repeated what his mother had told Millie when she'd asked the same question in the fall. "They're well fed. There are lots of deer around here. It's been a good year for the wolves."

"Not so good for the deer," Marc muttered, only half reassured.

In any case, the sinister howling was now coming from behind them. They went on their way again, keeping such a fast pace that it looked as if they were running away from something. Because they felt better hearing the sound of their own voices, the boys kept talking, even though they were out of breath.

"If my mom could see me, she'd have a fit," Marc snickered. "I phoned her at the hospital at noon. No kidding, mothers have radar. Three times she asked me if something was wrong."

"You didn't say anything?" asked Adam, worried.

"No. Well . . ." explained Marc, embarrassed, "to keep her from worrying I finally told her that . . . um . . . I was sick of staying with you."

Despite his exhaustion, Adam burst out laughing.

"Obviously it's not true," Marc protested. "Hey, the trick I played on my mom isn't all that funny. What's breaking you up so much?"

"Oh, listen. When my mother phoned me at five o'clock, just before we left, she thought I was hiding some problem from her. Mr. Jerome was breathing down my neck, listening to me, so I decided to give him an earful and went on and on about how you were getting on my nerves. And that's not true either. I'm so glad you're here with me. I'd be scared to death if I were all by myself."

Inwardly the two boys regretted their lies. Both of them wished they'd been able to tell about their escape plan. They wouldn't have felt so isolated. But then they'd have been forbidden to undertake the risky mission and would have been forced to disobey their mothers, which would hardly have been any better. Besides, they were on compulsory duty and Sixe had given them definite orders. Not anything, not anyone, could be allowed to jeopardize the success of Plan C.

After the path wound through a stand of cedars, the woods were suddenly gone. Gone, too, was the protection the trees provided against the elements. Gusts of wind now hit the boys full in the face, and as they panted and gasped, their breath rose like steam.

"There's the lake! Incredible! None too soon, either," puffed Marc, collapsing into a soft snowbank. "I'll never have enough strength to cross it."

The wind sharpened. Swirling blasts swept the surface of the frozen lake which was ringed by a dark band of gloomy evergreens. The leaden skies, without a star in sight, promised another snowfall.

"Come on," Adam urged, though he wondered whether he himself could find the courage to cover that last kilometre to the cottage.

He waved his mitten vaguely towards a bay on the other side of the lake. Through chattering teeth he tried to encourage his friend.

"We'll . . . b-build . . . a g-good . . . fire. And Cyber's there . . . w-waiting for us."

"We can't be sure about that," mumbled Marc, heaving himself up from the snowbank. He blamed the robot for launching them on this dangerous adventure in the first place. And as much as he'd dreaded the menacing woods behind them, he now feared the biting winds blowing across the lake.

Adam started down the steep bank, but misjudged his footing. The end of his snowshoe pierced the soft snow and he went headfirst down the embankment. His tuque, his glasses, and the flashlight went flying. Lying in the snow, Adam was on the verge of tears.

"My glasses, where are my glasses?" he cried, searching around frantically. It was no use. The glasses and the flashlight were buried and couldn't be found.

Marc yanked his chum to his feet and

helpfully, but roughly, brushed the snow off him. He held out Adam's tuque.

"Here. Put this back on. Whether we like it or not, we've got to keep going. We've come too far to think of going back. I'd like to tell that lousy Cyber of yours a thing or two . . . and give him a knuckle sandwich."

"That's an expression I don't know," said a serious voice behind them.

"Yikes!" roared Marc, nearly jumping out of his skin.

"Cyber! My good old silver Cyber!" Adam gasped.

"Welcome to Round Lake," Sixe declared gravely. "I observed a negative adjustment in your thermal state. Can I help you?"

"If you mean that we're frozen, you're absolutely right," growled Marc bitterly.

The robot instantly lit up, becoming white-hot and spreading a healing warmth around him. The green rays from his eyes grew brighter, turning into powerful beacons that made the desolate landscape look almost cheerful.

"Come. I will lead you."

"My glasses! I can't go without my glasses," Adam cried.

The robot's arm stretched over the area, waved from side to side, and then pushed down into the snow. Finally it reappeared with the glasses.

"While you're at it," Marc snapped, "find my flashlight."

Cyber did exactly that, and then led them across the lake. The journey seemed amazingly swift to the boys because the robot's rays had warmed them—and because now the end was in sight.

An hour later, seated before the roaring fire that Adam had promised, and with a steaming bowl of soup in front of them, the boys forgot all about their fears and fatigue. They were thrilled with their success.

"A cinch!" boasted Marc. "I said from the beginning that the trip would be peanuts for us. We're pretty amazing. I'd do it all over again right now if we had to. Fantastic!"

"No, Marc Aurèle. What we must do now is stay here until the victory."

"Now that we're out of the woods," Adam joked, nudging Marc with his elbow, "what should we be doing, Cyber? We're at your command."

"Speak for yourself," grumbled Marc.

But in the days that followed he came to see that, whether he liked it or not, he too was under orders from Commander Sixe of Amandara Tetra.

"Telephone for you, dear," shouted Mrs.

MacIntosh who seemed to think everyone was deaf.

Eve spoke very softly. "Yes, Aunt Corinne. In half an hour? I'll be ready. It's really nice of you to drive me to my music lesson. See you soon."

The little girl was playing her part thoroughly. On TV the enemies always bugged telephone calls. Even if the enemies in this case were the police, their faithful protectors, Eve and her aunt weren't taking any chances. Tefla had been firm: absolute secrecy.

Twenty minutes later Eve slipped into her red coat, snatched up her music case, and said goodbye to Mrs. MacIntosh. The blond young man with the hornrimmed glasses was at his post, sitting on a straight-backed chair, a book in his hand and his walkie-talkie in his pocket. Eve walked casually past the door to the service stairway and pressed the button for the elevator.

"Where are you going, sweetheart?" asked the security agent.

"To my piano lesson. My aunt's picking me up—she'll be waiting downstairs."

"You'd better not go out. There's going to be another power failure, and we won't be able to protect you out there in the dark."

"But that's not supposed to happen till tonight," Eve protested as the elevator opened and closed again in front of her nose.

The young man with the glasses wouldn't budge. He was pleasant, but unyielding.

"Don't go out today, dear. It's not a good idea."

"But my aunt will be waiting for me."

"I'll call the other agent downstairs and tell him to let her know. She'd be better off staying indoors too."

The agent muttered some instructions into his walkie-talkie. Apparently submissive, Eve turned back, dragging her feet. But as soon as the apartment door was shut, her fiery temper got the upper hand. The poor music case went flying, and the furious little girl exploded. She borrowed Marc's favorite expressions and added a few dramatic remarks of her own.

"Incredible! This is the unrealest of the unreal! Everything's wrecked. I'm a prisoner—like the princess in the ivory tower. This is the end! It's a total loss!"

Sultan wisely kept his distance, but Nootka went over to Eve. The robot was worried. But neither Nootka nor Eve gave up easily.

Five minutes later the young man with the glasses interrupted his reading a second time, marking his place with his finger. The door to the Kevins' apartment had opened again. But the agent quickly went back to his book and immersed himself in the story when he heard the shrill voice of Mrs. MacIntosh calling out some last advice to Eve who could be heard practising the piano.

Today Mrs. MacIntosh was in such a hurry that she raced down the stairs instead of waiting for the elevator. With her huge tam-o'-shanter covering her ear and her scarf wound three times around her face, she clumped noisily down the stairs in her oversized boots. The agent went over to the stairwell and looked down. He caught a glimpse of the rounded shoulders of her greenish coat and her enormous handbag trimmed with Scottish plaid.

Fear of the blackout had given Mrs. MacIntosh wings. The young man went back to his seat. The piano could be heard behind the closed apartment door. The little girl was practising.

But it was actually the robot who was giving the concert and who had imitated the housekeeper's farewells. The real Mrs. MacIntosh was totally unaware of the impersonation. She was busy in the kitchen, poking her head into the cupboards. Eve had told her she'd seen a ·cockroach in the breadbox. As far as Maggie MacIntosh was concerned, the search wouldn't be over until the vile creature had been found and exterminated.

Nootka played one last chord—without ever having touched the piano. Then the robot moved over to the sliding doors that led to the balcony. A familiar humming sound summoned Sultan who confidently followed his metallic friend. Gently the robot picked up the cat and gave it a hug. Sultan purred and half-closed his eyes, hypnotized by the vibrations.

Nootka planted herself by the balcony railing and waited. Two conditions were essential to the success of these new tactics. Corinne, forced to give up the project, would have to have resigned herself to parking in the underground garage. Then, Eve had to get down to the basement by way of the service stairway, without meeting the guards or attracting attention with her ridiculous disguise.

Both conditions were met. A few minutes later the little Volkswagen emerged from the entrance reserved for delivery vans at the back of the building. Were there any witnesses?

Without letting go of the cat, Nootka jumped into the air, floated over the balcony railing, and fell swiftly downward, stopping still about one foot from the ground. The car door opened and closed again. Sultan was scarcely aware of the mad leap that had brought him here. The car was already pulling quickly away. It swung past the building and raced down the street at high speed.

"Hey! That's our Volks!" cried the agent

keeping watch in his car at the front of the building.

He had just been starting to unwind, because chasing Corinne Kevin through the city traffic was always a hair-raising experience.

"Quick! Make a U-turn! She turned down Sixth Avenue!" exclaimed the second policeman.

"But which way has she gone now? Where'd she come from?" groaned the driver helplessly.

With a great deal of difficulty, the agents tailed the little red car as it led them in a mad chase towards the suburbs and then veered northeast. At the town of Squamish, Corinne turned resolutely northward, followed at some distance by her stubborn pursuers. She raced like a fireman on his way to a three-alarm call.

The physicist left the main highway and followed the side roads. Here and there they could see a few lights from the villages, the occasional logger's camp, or deserted house. Then suddenly, at seven o'clock, every light went out at once.

"There it is—it's started again."

Tefla didn't point out to them that this time it was for keeps. She didn't want to alarm her helpers. She wanted them to be clear-headed and calm. But in the eyes of a cosmonaut from a planet where all travel was done by air, this crazy obstacle course seemed very risky. Well, each world has its own way of doing things, she thought.

Eve, who'd long been accustomed to her aunt's flamboyant style, wasn't worried in the least. The little girl had shed Mrs. MacIntosh's outfit. Underneath it she'd worn her dark green snowsuit.

The Volks had reached an area that became more and more mountainous as they went on. Here, rain had not yet melted the heavy snows from the recent storms. Despite all of Aunt Corinne's tricks— speeding, driving with the headlights turned off, swerving on two wheels— she hadn't been able to lose the expert drivers who were right on her heels.

"It looks so easy on TV," she complained, discouraged. "The poorest amateur detective gets away with it."

The driver in the other car remarked sourly, "She's some driver, that physics professor. You'd think she was afraid her back wheels would catch up with her front ones. And she knows this area much better than I do."

His companion, holding on to his seat for dear life, meekly agreed. "An expert at drag racing. She's leading us to the end of the earth. We've turned our backs on civilization."

The two cars would soon come to the obscure little trail that wound around Black Mountain.

They would have to make a series of hairpin turns before they reached the top. Corinne had to do something quickly.

Once again Tefla suggested an extremely reckless solution. She was so persuasive that she managed to sweep away all obstacles and make the most improbable schemes sound possible. Eve trusted her totally and was ready for anything. Corinne, who'd been warned by David, resigned herself to the inevitable. The importance of their mission justified any kind of risk.

"Get ready! Only one more kilometre," announced the physicist, pushing the gas pedal to the floor. Her car leaped forward.

The pursuers were caught off guard. Driving more carefully because they didn't know the road, they began to speed up on a seemingly endless curve and had to brake suddenly when it turned at a forty-five degree angle.

They were relieved to be able to see the wild little car's tail lights in the distance. In their haste to catch up, they didn't even notice that they'd passed a small arrow pointing to the left that said, "Black Mountain, 6 kilometres."

Crouched at the foot of the little sign, Eve watched as the two cars sped into the distance and disappeared. Nootka had held onto her so firmly that she'd felt no shock at all when the robot hurled them from the moving vehicle. Now Aunt Corinne was leading the agents towards Pemberton, and they didn't know yet that their most important charges— Eve and her robot—were no longer in the red Volks.

Eve stood up and raised her eyes towards the gloomy shape of the mountain, feeling dwarfed by its hugeness. She peered into the dark but couldn't see anything, not even the roadway. The only sound was the great voice of the wind making mournful cries in the invisible treetops.

She knew that the cottage was located on the slope at the other side of the mountain, very near the top. It now seemed completely inaccessible. Eve's throat tightened, and a trembling sigh escaped her lips.

In a choked voice she whispered, "Are you there, Nootka? I'm a bit scared you know."

Immediately the filtered green rays lightly skimmed across the child's tense features.

"Trust me, Eve. I'm going to take you to the cottage. I'll lift you up and carry you the same way I carried Sultan. I'm very strong and I know exactly where to go. Are you ready? This will be your first rocket travel experience. It's a preparation for your future."

Presented in these terms, the flight seemed tempting. Eve felt herself being clasped and held tightly. Her feet left the ground, her face was lightly brushed by branches, and then she was above the forest, which slipped silently away beneath her.

"Close your eyes if you like," Tefla murmured gently.

"Are you kidding? Never! It's too exciting. I can feel the wind on my cheeks. You must be going really fast, Nootka."

Actually the robot was travelling almost too fast. The trip wasn't going to last long enough to suit Eve. They were close to the mountaintop. Eve guessed that they were skimming the rocky peaks.

Their descent down the other side was swift, ending in a dizzying dive towards the little camp, outlined against the north slope.

Now that her eyes had adjusted to the darkness, Eve could make out the silhouettes of the trees and the dull grey of the sky. With her mittens, she wiped away the tears that the wind and the speed had brought to her eyes.

What a marvellous flight! It was a pity she hadn't known before just what her robot was capable of doing. She'd have to describe the whole experience to her father. At the thought of the colonel, so far away and imprisoned, Eve felt a painful sadness.

"Have you got the key?" asked Nootka, shining a beam of light on the lock.

The inside of the cottage was dark and freezing cold. The Amandarian insisted that Eve carefully draw the heavy green curtains over the window before allowing the robot to provide heat and light.

Nootka explained, "A light would be seen from a great distance and, since the whole world has been plunged into darkness, we'll have to be discreet. Tonight I will keep you warm and give you light. Later on, we'll see. Are you hungry?"

"Yes. Daddy left some tubes of concentrated food—the kind they eat on board the rocket ships."

"You are beginning your apprenticeship in earnest. And after tomorrow, Eve, you are going to work very hard and very long without a break or a rest. All of my people are counting on you. You will take the place of your father who promised me his help. And at the same time you will be doing your part to give electricity back to Earth and to bring an end to the meteorological disasters."

"I don't know if I can do all that. Isn't Aunt Corinne going to help us?"

"Doctor Kevin will join us as soon as she manages to prove to her guards that they have no reason to watch her. They will be anxious to get back to their families during this state of alert, so we hope they won't insist on following her. But you, Eve, are the only one who knows how to help me."

"Me? I know how?"

"Yes. You understand the Amandarian language, and what you must do will resemble the game of Fala that I taught you—only this will be more complicated. Look."

A metal section in Nootka's middle slid open, just above the compartment that held the tools. Inside was a sophisticated instrument panel: twenty-five levers and keys of different colors ranged in rows of five, just like the pegs in the game of Fala. No one would ever have suspected the disturbing presence of this panel—neither the distrustful experts who'd gone over the robots' mysteries with a fine-toothed comb before allowing them to come to Earth, nor the unsuspecting children who owned them.

Tefla stroked Eve's hair. Her voice was gentle, spellbinding.

"Lie down now and go to sleep, my little friend. Tomorrow we have an enormous task to complete."

Eve wriggled submissively into a sleeping bag. Suddenly she looked up and said, "Nootka, I'd really like to talk to Adam. Is he going to help your planet too?"

"Yes. Adam and his friend Marc Aurèle are with Cyber inside the isolated cottage in the

Laurentians. But it's three o'clock in the morning there, and they must get their sleep. Don't worry, your friends are safe, as safe as anyone on Earth can be right now. Cyber spoke to me. You will talk to them tomorrow."

"Goodnight, Nootka. And goodnight, Tefla. I can picture you spinning out there and you can't see us because the whole earth is dark."

A small laugh came from Nootka's grille. "You are forgetting, my pet, that the sun is still lighting half of your planet. And in a few hours, it will shine on you too."

She soon went to sleep, bathed in the familiar green glow, and lulled by the voice of her far-off friend humming their favorite tune:

"Too ra loo, ra loo ral,
It's an Irish lullaby."

CHAPTER NINE

For twenty-four hours Earth had been without electrical power and without any communication systems.

The entire planet had been subjected to the worst storm that had ever battered it. Tidal waves ravaged the shores; in the forests, trees bent and shattered like glass; and the speed and violence of the gale-force winds increased daily.

Everywhere the people, plunged into darkness, gathered in groups and stayed below ground where it was safe, and tried to endure their trials with courage.

Hidden away in their underground shelter, the leaders of the United Governments now knew the real source of this menace. The star hurled into space by the implacable Worlaks swept aside everything in its path. Unable to help their people, the leaders realized, too late, that their only hope rested with the Green Planet.

Finally freed and pardoned, the two astronauts could do nothing but wait, powerless, hoping against hope that their families would be able to follow their very vague instructions.

The wind raged. It whirled the snow across the open surface of Round Lake and piled it up in huge banks whenever anything got in its way. The only cottage on its shores had virtually disappeared from sight under the huge snowdrifts. Then thin strips of yellow between the shutters were barely visible. Smoke unravelled from the chimney and was snatched away by the lashing winds.

The doorway to the log cottage was barred by a snowdrift as high as the door itself. In the safety of the cottage, two frightened boys meekly followed the instructions given by the little robot that had been their toy for so many months. Commander Sixe's unemotional voice clearly explained the world situation. Faced with its seriousness, even the rebellious Marc was subdued.

With the robot's help, the boys formed a production line and filled the one room of the cottage with every piece of wood they could find outside.

"All this? Unreal! You're not serious. There's enough here to heat a whole army camp," Marc complained. He wasn't fond of chores.

"Yes, all of it," Cyber flatly insisted. "Soon you won't be able to go out anymore. The wind will get worse and the temperature will drop. Make sure that the window on the north side will open easily. We must have a way of getting out, in case of danger."

"Incredible! When your uncle christened us the slaves of Round Lake, he wasn't kidding," Marc grumbled. He was prying the worm-eaten window frame with the poker. "Amazing! There now, we've got our emergency exit. Ooof!" he added, pulling his head back quickly as the wind took his breath away. "It'd take a real emergency to get me out there in this blizzard."

"But couldn't you keep us warm, Cyber?" Adam asked alarmed.

"There will soon be many other things for me to do. But don't worry, I won't leave you. Now then, Marc Aurèle, fill every container we have with snow. You must not be without water."

"Why me?" complained the neighbor. This was his final rebellion.

"Because Adam and I must begin our work. From now on, don't ask me for anything. Obey me instantly, just as you will have to do when you are space cadets at the Flight School."

The voice coming from the robot's grille was curt, authoritarian, unbending. This last argument broke down Marc's resistance. Like his friend, he was on active duty. Before long there were pots, pans, kettles, and plastic bags full of snow lined up at the back of the room near the frozen water pump.

Marc was also in charge of heating the cottage and preparing the meals. On Cyber's advice, they had closed off the fireplace which would have burned too much wood. They were using the little potbellied stove that stood in the middle of the floor.

"We're ready to withstand a siege," Adam observed, not quite realizing that his joke was all too realistic.

"Call from Van-cou-ver for A-dam Col-bert," the original electronic voice of Cyber suddenly announced. But it was in the new Cyber's tone of authority that they were then advised, "Be brief. Fi-nal com-mu-ni-ca-tion with Van-cou-ver."

The boys approached the robot. A tiny voice, trying to sound firm, came to them from the grille.

"Adam? Marc? Can you hear me? What are you doing?"

While Adam was saying hello, Marc interrupted him to complain bitterly, "We've got ourselves mixed up in Plan C."

"You too? Did you get a message in Amandarian?"

Quickly, the three friends exchanged their latest news. The boys, who counted so much on each other, were horrified to learn that Eve was completely alone with her robot. They didn't know that Tefla was as much comfort to Eve as Marc was to Adam.

"Aunt Corinne promised she'd come here."

"In this storm?" cried Marc before his friend had a chance to stop him from blurting it out.

Actually Eve needed encouragement, not pessimism. She hesitated, and when she spoke, her voice sounded less confident.

"The cottage is on the west side of the mountain. The wind's not as strong on this side . . . at least I don't think it is. That's what daddy told me."

"Who's looking after your stove?" asked Adam who sounded worried.

"We have oil heating here, and our tank is full. Daddy took care of that."

"Some people have unbelievably good ideas," sneered Marc sarcastically, throwing a dirty look at his stove which devoured wood all the time.

"Have you got any food? Who cooks it for you when you have to be at work with your robot?" Adam grinned at his own cook who was looking very pleased with himself.

Eve continued, "I have tubes of food—like the astronauts use. It's really easy 'cause you don't have to cook it." And then, just when the boys were envying her this sophisticated food, she added, "But it's not very good."

Cyber's lights began flashing rapidly to signal the end of the conversation.

Quickly Adam cried, "Good luck, Eve! Work hard."

"It's unreal how brave you are to stay there all by yourself," shouted Marc who got an elbow in the ribs for being so brutally frank.

"Bye, Marc! Farewell, Adam! You're my friend . . . forever and ever," replied the faraway voice. "Over and out," she added so faintly that they could hardly hear it.

"Her friend forever," said Adam dreamily. Then he looked up and asked anxiously, "Marc, did you think Eve was crying at the end?"

"Hey, don't be dumb. Of course not! She's too . . . too . . . solid to act like a baby. Just the same, I wouldn't want to be in her shoes, all alone with . . . *that.*"

Marc pointed disrespectfully at the robot. Cyber's eyes had turned green to end the children's conversation, but they now became blue to signal the start of serious work. A shrill whistle burst from the grille. Cyber gestured firmly with his arm, ordering Adam to come to him.

Adam pushed a low table up to the leather armchair. The robot stood on it in front of him. All at once a door slid open in the robot's stomach, revealing an instrument panel just like the one that had already amazed Eve.

"Wow!" said Adam, blinking his eyes behind his glasses. "You've been hiding things from me, old boy."

Apart from the twenty-five levers and the many numbered controls and keys, the robot had two control buttons on either side of his waist. With his pincers, he began to make some delicate adjustments. Cyber looked a bit silly in this position, like a plump little man with his hands on his hips.

Adam had seen plenty of proof that the pincers at the ends of those extended arms were very skilful, and was just about to ask the robot what sort of help a mere boy could offer. The green rays constantly sweeping across Adam's face must have read this question, because Commander Six began to explain in his friendly voice:

"I must keep adjusting the wave-length all the time."

"Will you tell me then, what I have to do?" urged Adam. A methodical mind and a thirst for knowledge were a space pilot's most precious gifts, and Adam had both.

"You will help me to determine the flight path of the star-missile. What we must do is direct the barrage of rays that our space fleet will use to attack it."

"Ultra-incredible!" gasped Marc, impressed. "Can I help too? I know how to play Fala."

Adam's friend tactfully failed to add that he was also better at math. But he wasn't too pleased with the Cinderella role he'd been given.

"Thank you, Marc Aurèle. But from now on all communications will be in Amandarian because the data will be coming directly from our ships."

Marc was following all these developments with keen interest and, to his great disappointment, Commander Sixe began to speak in his own language:

"As you see, Adam, the panel operates on the same principle as that of the Fala board. We invented it with the astronauts' help so that you and Eve could become familiar with its workings and calculations. I can't explain further; it would be too complicated. Be satisfied to obey blindly, keep calm, and pay close attention. I'll try to let you rest as often as possible, but this is war and you are a soldier. Don't forget that. Never take a break without my permission. Have you any questions?"

Adam, who'd never spoken a word in the language of the Green Planet, was utterly amazed to hear himself using exactly the right accent and perfect pronunciation.

"What should I do if I don't understand an order?"

"In that case, say 'negative.' And if further instructions still don't make it clear, say 'double negative'. We'll begin gradually and you'll have time to get used to the terms. When my rays are blue you'll be on duty. Green means 'at ease'. But if they ever start turning red, you and your friend must not go near the robot under any circumstances, and you must get as far away as possible. Understood? Repeat my instructions, Adam Colbert."

The youngster did so, as faithfully as he could.

"Very good. Now, repeat after me the name, number, color, and function of each lever on the panel. Turn every key to 'ACTION' and announce clearly each move you make. You must learn the maneuvers and the terms, and use the brief, impersonal tone of technical language. On with it."

At first Adam stammered and hesitated. He was afraid of making a mistake and as he'd always done, he looked for support from his friend. He kept trying to catch Marc's eye, but little by little he became absorbed in his new work. And then, when he heard approval in Commander Sixe's voice, he gained confidence.

For two hours Marc stared open-mouthed at this new Adam whose self-assurance was growing by the minute. He heard his friend's clipped tone, speaking in a strange dialect. As Adam's fingers grew more nimble and precise, they began flying over the multicolored keys, while the signal lights on the control panel flickered on and off.

Stronger and smarter, young Harel had always been the leader. It was with sincere admiration that he watched his once shy and protected friend turning into a clever and capable space cadet.

Finally Sixe's eyes became green. Satisfied with his pupil's progress, he announced, "Sixty minutes rest. Eat something and relax."

"Yes, Commander."

Adam stood at attention and saluted. He felt as if he were already at the Flight School. Then he blushed and turned to his friend, expecting to be teased. But Marc was staring at him with respect.

To cover his embarrassment, Adam gave his pal a shove and shouted, "It's freezing in here! What's the matter with the janitor?"

"Oh, unreal! I let the fire go out," cried Marc, stamping his feet. "You made me forget my chores with your sound and light show."

"Cadet Harel, you're under arrest!" joked Adam, wondering if Marc had also felt the call-to-arms and the sense of duty that had inspired him.

Marc raised his fist in the air and pointed his thumb skyward in the space pilots' salute.

"In future I'll be more careful, captain."

Adam grinned, feeling reassured. As usual, his friend didn't need to have everything spelled out. Once again they'd both had the same thought at the same time.

They relit the fire, opened some cans, and looked into the contents of the metal box outside the cottage where Uncle Alex had stored frozen foods. They pulled their sleeping bags close to the stove and refilled the oil lamps.

"We'd better use only one lamp at a time," Marc decided. He was taking his job as camp supervisor seriously. "Who knows how long we'll have to be here."

The two frightened boys didn't dare look at each other. Was this really the end of the world? Would they ever see their families again? The wind that shook the little house and threatened to blow its sloping roof off made them feel more stranded than the power failures afflicting the entire globe.

And Cyber, the familiar little robot whose presence was a sign of security and comfort, had become a heartless machine, withdrawn and single-mindedly concentrating on its serious technical problems. As if to confirm this, the green rays turned blue, a sharp whistle called Adam back to his place, and without any preamble, the commander began to give orders in his cold voice.

"Coordinates two blue, six red, twice left, three times nine, black."

"Negative," interrupted the technician who was afraid he'd missed one of the steps.

The unsympathetic voice repeated with machine-like precision, "Three times nine, black."

"Affirmative," replied Adam eagerly.

"Calculate at four different readings—blue nine, red twelve . . ."

All evening long, without a break, numbers and orders came from the impersonal grille. Adam's arms were weary, his eyes were crossing, stifled yawns stuck in his throat. He had to make a terrific effort to concentrate.

Marc had stayed up a long time just out of sympathy for Adam, but he finally fell asleep. Whenever Adam yelled out that he was cold, Marc would get up automatically and put another log on the fire, but then he'd dive back, shivering, into his sleeping bag. Adam was huddled in his own sleeping bag, even though he'd collected every sweater in the house and put them all on, one on top of the other.

Every once in a while Marc would feel sorry for Adam and heat some of the melted snow to make a bowl of soup or a cup of instant hot chocolate for his friend. Pale and drawn, Adam would smile his thanks without taking his eyes from the flashing lights.

Less and less Marc envied his friend's work which only a few hours before he'd wanted to do himself.

When the cold woke Marc at dawn, he saw that Adam was still in his chair, fast asleep with his head on his chest and his glasses down over his nose. The lamp had gone out and only the pale light coming through the shutters announced the arrival of another stormy day.

Perched on his table, a green-eyed Cyber was very slightly moving first one arm, and then the other, which he comically kept glued to his waist. Marc tried to imagine the incredibly complex network of circuits and relays by which such a small device could communicate with the stratosphere and regulate firing positions.

As Marc threw some logs into the stove, he scolded it: "You're unbelievable! Your appetite's worse than Zabulon's. If only you were as smart as he is, you could let me know when you're getting hungry and you wouldn't sit there all the time with an open mouth and frozen feet."

With a blanket wrapped around him like a cape, the cook measured some oatmeal into cold water, just the way his mother had taught him. But when breakfast was ready, he didn't have the heart to wake his chum, so he kept Adam's porridge warm in the top of the double boiler and waited.

Outside the storm was still raging. It was impossible to see where the earth ended and the sky began, for the blizzard bathed everything in a depressing grey light. This was not the way Marc had pictured the end of the world. He'd have preferred great thunderbolts or a blazing sun.

The cottage began to warm up. Marc didn't dare light the lamp for fear of waking Adam. He lay down again with his arms behind his head and thought things over. He wasn't especially proud of the role he'd played so far. From now on he'd have to organize ways to keep his friend from being cold and hungry and means of making his difficult work easier.

He thought of Eve who had to face these frightful hours at the top of a mountain all alone!

CHAPTER TEN

Before she even opened her eyes, Eve asked lazily as she did every morning, "Nootka, what's the weather like?"

Usually the robot answered automatically and reeled off a scientifically precise weather report. It was more to hear a friendly voice than to learn the temperature that Eve asked this question. But today, when the little girl needed friendship more than she ever had, she got no answer.

Worried, she sat up quickly. Had she been abandoned on this mountainside in the midst of a howling storm?

The green curtains covered every window. Blasts of wind shook the cottage, even though it was partially protected by the huge bulk of the mountain behind it. The darkened room was warm and cosy.

Where was Nootka? Why didn't she answer? Through the gloom Eve could just make out the silver form of the robot whose green rays seemed to be fastened on the glowing stove. Reassured, Eve lay back on her pillow and began to laugh.

"Do you ever look funny, Nootka, with your hands on your hips that way. You look like Mrs. MacIntosh when she dances her Scottish jigs for me. Are your eyes green? Anyway, I see that you're working too hard to answer me. That's okay. As long as you're there, that's good enough for me."

With a shiver the little girl wriggled out of her sleeping bag and placed her bare feet on the ice-cold floor.

"Wait just a few minutes. I'll get dressed, and after breakfast we'll work together. It'll be even more exciting than playing Fala. I hope you'll be pleased with me."

Talking the whole time, Eve pulled on her woollen slacks, thick socks, and two sweaters. She opened the curtains and made a face at the dreary light coming through the windows. The normally magnificent landscape had been blotted out by the blinding snow. And the feeling of crushing loneliness was heightened by the constant wailing of the incredibly violent winds.

Without waiting for answers to her monologue, the little girl went on talking to the robot. She felt less alone hearing a human voice, even though it was only her own. She carefully rolled up her sleeping bag because, under Nootka's guidance, she'd grown tidier during the past few months.

She refilled the gas in the lamp and then lit it to brighten the depressingly grey day. Eve now understood why her father had insisted on teaching her how to handle these lanterns. There were three more of them lined up on a shelf. By lighting them one after the other, she'd have light for hours—even days and nights, if necessary. That thought discouraged her, so she pushed it firmly out of her mind.

Nootka must have lit the stove during the night because heat was coming from it. Eve made a quick astronaut's breakfast. She placed a plastic tube containing a mixture of cream of wheat and milk into a special container. With one push of a button the porridge heated instantly. By inserting a big straw into the cylinder, she could gulp down the hot, sweetened cereal. It was fun to eat the way her dad and the rocket ship pilots did on their space voyages. As Nootka had remarked the night before, Eve's training as a flight cadet was beginning right now.

Eve brought a chair over to the table where

she'd arranged all the lamps and the matches. She laid out dozens of tubes of the concentrated food. Despite all the efforts made to season and vary these meals, actually eating them was a lot like swallowing toothpaste of different colors. It wasn't always very appetizing.

The little girl piled some cushions and blankets in the armchair and checked to see if she had everything she needed. She brought a pitcher of water, some picture books, and Aunt Corinne's travel alarm clock. Finally she placed a chair in front of the armchair. Everything was all set.

"You can come now, Nootka. I'm ready."

But the silent, stationary robot didn't react. Fortunately Tefla had explained this apparent indifference to Eve the night before:

"Sometimes all my attention will be concentrated on my calculations and I won't be able to talk to you. When the robot is relaying our communications or intercepting the enemy's fleet, all its circuits will be busy. Then Nootka won't be able to provide heat, or obey you, or even transmit my messages. I'm warning you now so you won't feel neglected.

"I'll try to come back as often as possible, my dear. But you will have to realize the gravity of the situation and the danger to your planet and mine. Your role will be important—essential—

because you will do what Colonel Kevin would have done. You'll have to be as strong, as brave, and as patient as your father."

"I understand. I'll do my best," Eve promised.

All the same, Nootka's stubborn silence hurt Eve. She'd wanted compliments for her excellent planning. But then she became resigned and told herself that at the Flight School they wouldn't praise the cadets every time they did something well, even though they'd probably point out their mistakes right away. Maybe she really had led a pampered life and wasn't prepared for the future she wanted. Here was a good chance to begin her apprenticeship.

Eve picked up one of the picture books and plunged into the adventures of Asterix. These were old books that had become popular again. At Adam's suggestion, she had bought them in the original French. After a while the words and pictures began to blur, and cadet Eve Kevin fell asleep with her nose in her book.

A touch on her shoulder startled her awake. Nootka was perched on the chair in front of her, staring at her with the green rays and stroking her hair with an outstretched arm.

"You've done a wonderful job of preparing everything we'll need for the next few hours, my pet. Are you ready to get to work?"

"Yes, I'm ready. But isn't Aunt Corinne going

to come?"

The robot turned towards the window.

"My sensors do not detect her presence. And the atmospheric conditions . . ."

"You mean she won't be able to get up the mountain in this storm?"

"It's quite possible."

Tefla was suddenly interrupted. The rays turned blue and a short whistle called the girl and her robot to attention.

"To work, Eve Kevin. Two black on three red, left twice. Got that?"

"Affirmative."

During the series of instructions that came from Nootka's grille, Tefla had less and less time to break in with personal remarks. Very soon the familiar voice was replaced by the curt orders of an unknown Amandarian. Even though she was frightened, Eve managed to follow orders.

The rocket ship pilots out there very likely didn't know that their technician on Earth was a solitary young girl. It never occurred to them to treat her gently. But maybe the gravity of the situation wouldn't permit them to?

Hour after hour with very few interruptions, Eve continued. By nightfall her arms were tired, her back ached, and she felt like yawning all the time. When the green lights signalled a rest, Tefla's preoccupied voice offered a suggestion.

"You're very tired. Heat a cylinder of coffee."

"But that'll keep me awake," Eve protested without thinking.

All at once the distant Amandarian and Eve shared one of the joyous laughs that made their friendship so special.

"Am I ever dumb, Tefla! That's exactly why you offered me coffee. I think Aunt Corinne would let me have it, just this once."

Mention of the physicist upset Eve, but a new summons to work interrupted her sad thoughts. The coffee kept her going for another two hours, but then, just as the blue lights went out, Eve felt her eyes closing in spite of herself.

"Sleep, my little pet," Tefla murmured. "You've certainly earned it."

Suddenly the robot turned its head sharply towards the door. Eve was startled and her heart pounded.

"What's the matter? Did you hear something?"

"I detect the approach of a vehicle on the road that goes around the mountain."

"In this wind? Is it the police?"

Eve didn't realize how strange this reaction seemed.

All of a sudden she looked upon the police as enemies, when before they had been her protectors.

Fearfully the little girl went to the window and

looked out into the valley. Rain was coming down in torrents; the visibility was zero. Who would dare to be on that dangerous road in such weather? She looked questioningly at her robot. The tortured expression on her pale face showed how frightened she was.

Nootka joined her by the window and pointed an arm towards the door.

"The car has stopped. It has no more fuel. The driver is getting out and is coming on foot. I detect the presence of a second creature."

"Creature?" exclaimed Eve, terrified. "What kind of creature? Tefla, I'm scared."

The little girl impulsively threw herself into the robot's arms. Much to her surprise, a little giggle came from the grille.

"Don't be afraid, my pet. The first creature is your Aunt Corinne. The second . . ."

A shriek of anguish interrupted this news.

"Aunt Corinne! She'll kill herself trying to climb the mountain in this weather. Nootka, please, *please* go and meet her. Help her the way you helped me. Quick, quick!"

With all her strength Eve pulled at the robot which seemed to be bolted to the floor. Eve was so impatient that she kicked the robot, which had no affect on the metal surface but hurt her own toes instead.

"I cannot leave my post, Eve. The fate of your

world depends on my staying here."

Eve was beside herself with worry. She kneeled before Nootka so she could look directly into the green eyes.

In a trembling voice she asked, "Does the fate of the world depend on my help too?"

"Yes, Eve. It's essential."

The little girl sat back on her heels, firmly crossed her arms and, defiantly thrusting out her chin, announced, "Then that's just too bad for the world! 'Cause if you won't go and get Aunt Corinne, I'm not going to help you any more!"

After a few moments of stunned silence, Tefla's gentle voice replied, "Very well, mistress. As you wish. I will advise my leaders of this ultimatum and I will obey you."

The door opened and shut again, letting a blast of wind and rain into the cottage. Drenched and chilled, Eve went to the stove and reached with shivering hands for its comforting warmth. Tears of anxiety streamed down her cheeks. She waited and waited. What were her Aunt and Nootka doing out there in the storm?

At last a light flickered through the gloom. It vanished, then reappeared, closer. The robot's powerful beams loomed suddenly, three metres above the ground. A dark shape could be seen underneath.

Eve opened the door and was immediately flattened against the wall by the force of the blast. The lamp blew over and its glass cover fell to the floor. Curtains and papers were sent flying by the wind. A sound close to Eve told her that she wasn't alone. Bracing herself against the door, she tried to push it shut. A sturdy arm helped her and the door finally closed.

The roaring tempest was followed by silence. The little girl rushed to her aunt who lay stretched out, soaking wet, on the floor. Doctor Kevin gradually began to catch her breath. With her straggly hair, her dirt-smeared face, and her scratched chin, she looked like someone who had truly been exposed to the raging elements. But even her dripping backpack didn't prevent her from reaching out her arms to her niece who fell into them laughing and crying at the same time.

"Aunt Corinne! You're safe! Am I ever glad to see you!"

"My little Eve," Corinne puffed, out of breath. "At last! I'm with you again. I was frantic with worry. Are you all right? You look peaked and worn-out."

"Did you get away from the police?"

"No, they caught up with me at Pemberton. They were pretty upset when they couldn't find you or your robot. I refused to tell them where you were."

"They didn't torture you, did they?"

"You've seen too many movies, my pet. Those policemen were there to protect us. They very politely asked me to stay overnight in a motel and then locked me in a room on the second floor while they guarded the exit."

Aunt Corinne took off her soaked knapsack and stood up with great dignity.

"It never occurred to them that I could escape through the window. A mountain-climbing physicist should never be confused with an old invalid who sits by the fire and knits. Speaking of fire . . . ," Aunt Corinne continued undoing the straps of her knapsack and opening one of the flaps, "I know somebody else who'd like to get warmed up too."

Sultan's silky head emerged from its hiding place. The cat stretched in a stately manner, jumped down, and began purring and rubbing against his young mistress's legs. Then he went off to inspect his new home. Eve burst out laughing.

"Is that who it was? The second creature Nootka told me about?"

"I owe a debt of gratitude to your robot, my love. Without her, I'm sure the wind would have finished off what the rain began, and I'd have gone down that mountain a lot faster than my little rattletrap ever could have climbed it."

"Did you run out of gas?"

"Halfway to the top. Thanks to the power failure, the gas pumps at the service stations weren't working. I managed to siphon a few litres from the tank of the car that chased us. We saw that trick on a police show last month, remember?"

"Aunt Corinne, you'd make a great gangster," Eve sighed, hugging her warmly.

The physicist didn't mention all the terrible dangers she had survived. Roads had been flooded and threatened by uprooted trees and falling rocks. Only her determination to be with her niece had given her the courage to continue her daring trip.

Corinne Kevin was herself again. She got up, lit one of the lamps, and slipped a tube of coffee into the heater. Intrigued because her niece who was usually such a chatterbox was so quiet, she turned and saw that the little girl had fallen asleep on the edge of the sofa.

The robot spread a blanket over Eve and whispered to the worried physicist, "The work that we are demanding from this child is very hard, but she understands the necessity. An hour from now she will have to begin transmitting again."

"I'll help her," Corinne promised. "Even if I

don't know Amandarian, I can certainly make some calculations."

So it was a very determined trio who went to work as soon as the robot gave its urgent whistle sixty minutes later. Days and nights passed. No one cared about time in the little rustic house battered by the gale. All over the storm-wracked planet, terrified people awaited the end of the world.

CHAPTER ELEVEN

Adam and Marc were so worn-out that it took them a moment to notice that Cyber's blue beams had abruptly gone out. Adam's arm was hanging heavily at his side. He leaned back in his chair to enjoy this break. He had been working almost non-stop for the past few days. His head drooped and he fell asleep.

Marc reluctantly slipped another log into the stove. His supply of wood was diminishing in an alarming way. Outside the temperature continued to fall and the constantly swirling snowstorms made it impossible to tell the sky from the ground.

Morale in the log cabin was at its lowest, but the boys didn't let up on their gruelling task. Marc was conditioned to know exactly when to heat the stove, fill the lamps, or offer soup, sandwiches, or hot chocolate to his friend. Like a robot, Adam followed the instructions given by Commander Sixe and the other space pilots from the Amandarian fleet.

There was no way of assessing the results of all these efforts. Cyber didn't have a spare second to send personal messages from Sixe.

As he stirred the embers to rekindle the flame, Marc watched the stationary robot. Even its arms hung motionless and, for the first time since he'd known the robot, Cyber wasn't staring with those bright rays as he usually did.

Could the robot be dead? Had it lost contact with the satellite that gave it its heart? Was their mission accomplished at last, and the demanding robot merely letting Adam have a little rest? Marc resented Commander Sixe and all the other tyrants who'd made his friend work so hard for days on end.

Suddenly the boy straightened up, all his senses on the alert. Cyber's lights had come on, but this time the rays were red and menacing. The steel pincer pointing at the sleeping boy could have been dangerous too.

Marc grabbed the poker and sprang towards the table where Cyber was perched. As he shoved the table sharply, it overturned with a crash. Adam was so exhausted that he didn't even open his eyes.

The robot floated in the air. Marc slipped between Cyber and Adam. Brandishing the poker aggressively, Marc roared, "Don't you dare touch my friend, you lousy power-driven cooking pot! I've got a can opener here that'll split your tin head wide open. Keep your paws off him!"

Marc knew very well that Cyber could paralyse him or even kill him. But there was no way he was going to let a robot endanger the life of his best friend. Bravely the boy placed himself between the two, defying the potentially fatal rays.

Cyber withdrew his pincer and, in a faint, faraway sounding voice, said, "Marc Aurèle, my friend, you are extremely courageous. I wanted to say a final farewell to my master, Adam. Thank him for me . . . and . . ."

Marc had to strain to hear the end of the faltering message.

" . . . and on . . . behalf of my . . . people. I . . . must leave . . . and . . . transmit all . . . the data . . . that has . . . been . . . calculated. Over . . . out . . . urgent . . ."

Slowly, as if all its powers had been exhausted, the robot swivelled towards the back wall of the cabin. Marc raced to the window and flung the shutters open. As Cyber passed in front of him and slipped through the opening, the silver metal had already begun to redden and give off an alarming heat.

Marc watched the red beams travelling over the clouds of snow, saw them diminish and then vanish around the corner of the house. The boy drew in his head and carefully shut the window. A lump came to his throat as he thought of the glowing little robot on its way to fulfil its final duty. He was acutely aware of the bonds of friendship that had developed between them.

Adam was slipping off his chair. Marc rushed to pile some cushions on the floor underneath him. He wrapped Adam in his sleeping bag, took off his glasses, and covered him with several blankets. Adam slept through it all.

Marc put more wood on the fire. He was too tired to think of tomorrow. The only thing he wanted in the whole world was to lie down and forget about the past days and nights.

Still the wind howled, blowing away the chimney smoke. Beneath the sloping roof hooded with snow, the children slept. Before long the lamp ran out of fuel and went dark. The day drew to a close; night drifted in.

By the lake, an intermittent bright light marked the spot where an Amandarian robot tirelessly transmitted information to a space fleet — information that would intercept, and later destroy, the black ships of the Worlaks.

All around this source of intense heat the snow darkened and melted, as if consumed by a raging inferno.

Another day began. Gradually the snowstorm let up, then stopped completely. The wind dropped, and little by little the temperature began to climb. Inside the shrouded cottage there was neither light nor smoke to signal the presence of human life.

The roar of a powerful engine shattered the silence of Black Mountain. The snow tires gripped the surface of the bumpy road, whole sections of which had slid away to the bottom of the slope. At a bend in the road, an abandoned little red Volkswagen blocked the way. Its hood lay in the muddy ditch, its doors hung awry, twisted by the wind.

"That's my sister's car!" cried the colonel as he jumped down from the Land Rover. "They made it this far."

The soldiers who were with the astronaut looked skeptically at the steep mountainside. How could a woman and a little girl have managed to survive and reach the cottage which was perched up near the summit?

Pale sunlight lit the scene of devastation. What had once been a fertile valley spread out at the foot of Black Mountain was now a tableau of landslide scars, washed-out bridges and roofs torn off by the fierce winds. In fact, this was a sight that could be seen all over the world. With the return of fine weather, everybody tried to forget about the wreckage and turned their attention instead to a future that was now filled with hope.

The rescue team resolutely started their climb. The officer in charge tried to keep the astronaut at the rear of the group. He had hoped to save the space hero from the possibility of discovering that his family was dead. But David Kevin wanted to be the first to reach the house.

"I found something," shouted one of the soldiers, stopping in front of a scorched boulder to pick up several pieces of blackened metal that had been twisted by fire. No one paid any attention to him. They had no time for scraps of metal.

The colonel's shout of triumph drew them towards the house. Through the door that he'd just opened, a ray of sunlight fell on a touching sight. Corinne Kevin and her niece who was hugging their cat, lay fast asleep in each other's arms.

Eve opened her eyes first and discovered her father bending over her. The little girl gently pushed Sultan aside. Filled with emotion, the colonel tenderly lifted up his daughter and they hugged and kissed each other.

"Daddy! You're not a prisoner anymore! And the sun is shining! Does that mean it's all over?"

"The nightmare's over, princess. Amandara saved us. The Worlak's space fleet has been wiped out and the killer-star's diverted!"

Eve's grey eyes suddenly filled with tears. Her lips trembled as she announced sadly, "Nootka's gone. Her eyes went red and she got burning hot. She said goodbye to me in a little weak voice, and she patted my hair and . . . and . . . she went out into the storm. I think . . . I think she's . . . dead, daddy."

"A robot doesn't die, my darling. It's a machine. But I can tell you that your friend Tefla is safe and well. She and Sixe returned to their flagship and are heading for Amandara Tetra with all the men and women from their victorious fleet. They sent us a message of gratitude as soon as communications with Earth were re-established. Thanks to them, and to your help and Adam's, their planet was saved—and our own too."

"Thanks to Nootka and Cyber, daddy. We mustn't forget them, even if they were only . . . only . . . m-m-machines."

Eve burst into tears on the colonel's shoulder. Her heart was breaking at the thought of her gallant little silver robot who'd gone out into the storm to save the world and, in doing so, had perished.

Corinne and her brother tried to comfort the heartbroken child. Then they began to get ready for their return to Vancouver. Sultan again complained loudly about his place in the depths of the backpack.

When it was time to leave, Eve insisted on locking up with her own key that she still had around her neck.

"We'll come back as soon as the road is fixed. But I wish you could have seen the way Nootka made me fly up to the top of the mountain, just like a bird."

"I can imagine it easily," said Corinne who'd had a taste of the same kind of transport when the robot had taken her up to the mountaintop in the storm.

"Poor little Nootka," Eve said again. "I never thought she'd have to give her life for us. Daddy, you mustn't say she was just a machine. To me, she was a friend."

"There it is—on the northwest side of the lake."

The big army helicopter skimmed the area that Captain Vimont had pointed out. They had to fly in close to spot the snow-covered cabin. The pilot looked around for a safe place to land.

"Look at the circle of melted snow in the bay," exclaimed one of the soldiers on the rescue team. "It looks like a landing strip made just for us."

The helicopter hovered noisily over the makeshift airstrip which showed a black spot at its center that was only partly covered with snow. That was all that remained of the robot. Its overheated circuits had consumed the metal and hollowed out a large dent in the ice.

Before the propellers stopped, a team of men armed with shovels began attacking the huge snowdrifts that reached the top of the cabin's roof. The worried astronaut noticed that there was no smoke coming from the chimney and there were no other signs of life. Had they arrived too late? Had the children been battling the cold for days? Because of his injuries, Alex Vimont couldn't help the rescue team. Instead he sent out Zabulon who'd been brought along in case his talent for hunting was needed to locate the boys.

"Come to the back!" cried one of the soliders. "We can open the shutters and call inside."

The opening wasn't large enough for a man to get through, and there was no answer when they called. Nothing moved inside the dark, bitterly cold cottage. Fortunately, however, the snow piled up on the roof and around the cottage had made an excellent windbreak.

By the light of the flashlights, all they could see were tuque pompons, sticking out of sleeping bags. No more logs were left in the cabin, and the broken remains of a chair showed that attempts—probably disappointing—had been made to burn some of the furniture.

Nothing they did could wake the children from their sleep: not the roar of the helicopter, not the banging on the shutters, nor the rescuers' shouts. The men with the shovels hurried to dig out the doorway.

But Zabulon couldn't wait any longer. He pushed furiously past the man at the window and bounded through the narrow opening. The dog threw himself upon the two sleepers, nudged them enthusiastically, lashed them with his tail, and began to lick their reddened noses and heavy eyelids. Finally he snatched Adam's hat off by the pompom, hoping for the chase that always followed this sort of trick.

His young master raised a tousled head and for the first time became aware of the repeated banging at the door.

"Hold on! Don't knock it down!" cried Adam who felt guilty enough about having tried to burn one of his uncle's chairs. Surely they wouldn't have to knock down the door as well.

Adam crawled out of his sleeping bag. Still sleepy, he walked unsteadily over to the door.

When he opened it he found himself face to face with policemen. Mr. Jerome was at the front, furious because the boys entrusted to his care had escaped.

When Marc opened his eyes, he saw that he was surrounded by soldiers with guns slung across their shoulders. As soon as he opened his mouth, he began to protest his innocence. Adam and Marc had been wondering for some time whether they might be sent to prison.

"Unreal! We didn't commit such a big crime. All we did was run away . . . and burn two legs of a chair."

But to their surprise, the soldiers who were now swarming into the dark cottage seemed to be treating Adam and Marc like heroes instead of criminals. Two male nurses with Red Cross badges on their sleeves were even unfolding stretchers so that the victims could lie down on them.

Adam and Marc protested strongly. Apart from feeling hungry, they were fine. Their long sleep had rested them and prevented them from feeling the piercing cold that surrounded the warm cocoon of their sleeping bags.

Adam began to look around, and asked Marc, "Where's Cyber hiding?"

"He went out the window while you were sleeping."

"You let him go out in the storm?"

"Listen, chum, you don't argue with Commander Sixe, or with a robot whose eyes are on fire. Anyway, it was time for Cyber to leave, 'cause he was burning hot and would have blown up in our faces."

"Oh, that must be very bad for his circuits," lamented Adam who refused to imagine the worst. "We've got to find him."

He headed for the door. Marc caught him by the arm and held him back. The solemn expression on his face gave away his feelings.

"Adam, this is too unreal for words. I don't know how to tell you, but I think your robot is . . . dead. Sending all those messages was too much for him."

Seeing his friend's grief-stricken look, Marc made a clumsy attempt at sympathy.

"That's why he came to Earth—to rescue us. He gave his life, just like a . . . little tin soldier. He wouldn't want you to go into mourning for him, for heaven's sake!"

"Let's hope Sixe is still alive," whispered Adam, blinking his eyes to keep from crying.

The officer in charge came over and advised the boys, "You'd better run out to the helicopter and let Captain Vimont see that you're all right."

Adam rushed past the walls of snow that framed the doorway. But Marc couldn't help stopping on the doorstep when he noticed the huge machine, its propellers sparkling in the sunlight.

"Wow! Are we going to be able to fly in that?"

"Certainly. We came here just to pick you up."

"To pick us up? A-ma-zing! Wait'll the gang hears that the army came just for us. . . ."

Suddenly worried, Marc turned to the officer who was making sure everything was in order before locking the cottage.

"Sir, are you going to explain to my parents that I . . . I mean that we . . ."

"Your parents know all about your adventure. They're proud of you. They're waiting at the airport with Captain Vimont's sister and his niece."

Full of excitement, the boys took their places inside the helicopter. The astronaut shook hands with them as if they were colleagues, and brought them up to date on Amandara Tetra's victory. He swiftly set their minds at ease about the world situation, the fate of their families, and that of their co-workers, Sixe and Tefla.

Alex Vimont congratulated them on their resourcefulness. And then, pretending to be outraged, he exclaimed, "Thank goodness we arrived before all my furniture was gone!"

"We only burned two little legs," pleaded Marc sheepishly.

"We were too tired to chop up the back of the chair with the axe," Adam explained.

Alex teased, "It sure was hard to wake you up. You almost slept till the end of the world."

Adam was able to top that by saying, "The Judgement Day trumpets would have wakened us." Like his uncle, he had a taste for black humor. "Marc would have heard them instantly."

"Hey, that's not something to joke about," said Marc with a shiver. "We came pretty close."

The helicopter took off, raising a terrific cloud of snow. In the very place where it had been, a little pile of twisted metal was embedded in the thawing snow. In the spring it would sink to the bottom of the lake, and there would be no further sign of the robot's brief visit to Earth.

Adam's nose was pressed against the window, but he couldn't see a single trace of Cyber's existence. From what his uncle said, the robot could not possibly have avoided self-destructing once his circuits had begun to overheat. With a heavy heart, the young master paid silent tribute to the one who'd been his constant companion for so many months.

CHAPTER TWELVE

"Montreal calling Vancouver. Montreal calling Vancouver."

"This is Vancouver. Go ahead."

"Can you hear me, Vancouver?"

"Loud and clear. All systems are go, Adam Colbert."

"Eve, do you really think we need to use this jargon?"

"No, but it's fun to imitate real astronauts."

"With Cyber and Nootka, we didn't need it."

"I know what you mean. I have the feeling too, that a whole bunch of people are listening in on our wave-length. That's why I'm speaking to you in English."

"Just the same, Eve, Uncle Alex said that the Air Ministry reserved a special frequency for us when they gave us these transmitter-receivers."

"It was pretty nice of them to try to replace our robots so we could still have our talks. It's much more fun that the phone."

"Or letters. Are you back at school?"

"Yes! The schools opened again today all over British Columbia. No more storms, and no more holidays. What about you?"

"It's the same in Montreal. It's strange, but math doesn't bother me at all anymore. You should use your French, Eve, if you don't want to forget it."

"You're right. I'm really glad about your math, Adam, because even though the Flight School promised to accept us, we'll have to pass the entrance exams. Daddy says that even if the government is grateful, they won't admit unqualified cadets. What's so funny, Adam Colbert?"

"I was just thinking that you've got quite a way to go with your French."

"Well, we'll speak nothing but French when your family comes to visit at Easter. Then I'll really learn."

"With Millie there, you'll have to. She speaks English about as well as they do in a silent movie."

"Adam, Aunt Corinne is going to drive us up to the cottage at Black Mountain. Will Marc be allowed to come with you?"

"He wouldn't miss it for anything, especially since he found out that we're going to travel in one of the Flight School's jets."

"That's great! Then it'll be my turn in the summer. Are you sure your mom won't mind my coming to Round Lake during the holidays?"

"Of course not. We'll get Marc to wash the dishes. He loves that."

"I do not!" yelled an indignant voice. "You guys are plotting behind my back."

"If you'd knock before coming in, you wouldn't take us by surprise," said Adam, very haughtily.

"Yeah, yeah, well I'm here now. No more little secrets."

"That's what you think," teased Eve.

And then she continued to speak, but in the melodious language of Amandara Tetra.

"You know something? I liked it much better when I listened to you through little Nootka's grille."

After a silence filled with memories, Eve went on, "Adam, did you hear that program last night, when the United Governments talked about the war between the planets?"

"Yes. They headed off the killer-star and it's now going to be lost in space. But the government didn't tell everything. It's weird, knowing information that's secret from the rest of the world."

"Daddy told me that he and your uncle insisted that we say nothing about what we did. He said that the publicity would drive us crazy afterward. We'd never get away from it for the rest of our lives."

Amandara Tetra and Earth had signed an official alliance. They'd exchanged ambassadors, and the first ones from Earth were Alex Vimont and David Kevin. Although the governments would have liked to express publicly their thanks to the children whose intervention had saved two civilizations, the parts played by Eve, Adam, and Marc would not be known for many, many years—at least not on Earth.

Their families had refused all such honors on the children's behalf. Instead they had received letters of thanks, a recommendation for admission to the Flight School, and scholarships. But the best reward of all was a promise that the three children would be the first civilians invited to visit Amandara Tetra in the years to come.

Eve and Adam were quite happy with this anonymity. It would have been very difficult to be an international celebrity and a student at the same time. Adam summed up their feelings philosophically:

"Anyway, it's as my mother says, what we did

was just a matter of circumstances. Other kids would have done the same thing if they'd been in our shoes."

"That's true. Adam, my dad's leaving tomorrow for Amandara Tetra. I'll really miss him while he's away for so many months."

"It'll go fast. And then you'll come to visit us. Uncle Alex is really glad to be going. The Amandarians will finish healing him there. He says he's going to leave them his cane for a souvenir."

"Is it true that Commander Sixe is going to make something for you that will fix your eyesight?"

"That's what he promised. After all that, if I don't become an astronaut, I won't have any right to go to Amandara."

"Tefla begged me not to forget their language. She said I should practise with you. You and I will be the ambassadors from Earth later on."

A loud noise coming through the speakers made Eve jump. She was so surprised that she stopped speaking Amandarian.

"What was that?"

"That's my nutty neighbor. He just played a note on his bugle, right into the speaker."

"What? Has he got a bugle?"

"Yes I have, miss," bragged Marc, pleased to be included in the conversation. "I've got a flute too. And I'm saving up for a trombone. I'll be able to play duets with you at your piano."

Adam was a bit jealous. He said sarcastically, "It'll sound really terrific when you play all three of them at once."

Eve broke in diplomatically, "Daddy says he's going to bring us some other robots when he comes back from Amandara. And there's going to be one for you, Marc."

Adam heaved a sigh of regret.

"They'll just be ordinary old robots that can catch a ball, or make beds, or go get us a glass of water. Nothing more than that."

"Well, that's not too bad," said Marc, satisfied.

Eve understood Adam's disappointment.

She answered softly, "But they won't have hearts, like Nootka and Cyber did. Those two were more than robots."

"They were friends," said Adam, "Our robot friends. . . ."